NIGHTMARE—OR WARNING?

Ahead he spotted something white caught in the main stream of the water channel. He thought it was a piece of cloth till he got closer, then it looked more like a drowned animal—a rabbit maybe, a cat, a bird perhaps; a white owl, though it had too much flesh on it to be a bird.

He was standing over it before he realized what he was staring at and stepped back in horror.

It was a human hand, severed just above the wrist.

OUIJA

**When the dead speak,
the living die.**

ouija

ANDREW LAURANCE

CHARTER/DIAMOND BOOKS, NEW YORK

OUIJA

A Charter/Diamond Book / published by arrangement with
the author

PRINTING HISTORY
Star Book edition published 1982
Charter/Diamond edition / November 1990

ISBN: 1-55773-415-1

Charter/Diamond Books are published by The Berkley
Publishing Group, 200 Madison Avenue, New York,
New York 10016. The name "CHARTER/DIAMOND"
and its logo are trademarks belonging to Charter
Communications, Inc.

PRINTED IN THE UNITED STATES OF AMERICA

10 9 8 7 6 5 4 3 2 1

CHAPTER ONE

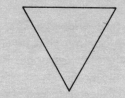

WARREN was sceptical.

Young Zuke believed it, and so did the more mature Chantal. They both consulted it and took advice from it, which was why all three of them were now stooping to go in through the low doorway of the small whitewashed house in the poorer quarter of the village.

Up till then it had all been quite amusing. Warren had gone along with the lunacy because he liked their company, just he alone for the last five days with these two attractive females. With these *three* attractive females! For there was Jacinta.

He hadn't expected to enjoy himself as much when he'd set off for Spain. The exhibition in

1

Puerto Lucena where he was representing his company had not held the promise of anything exceptional. A few hours a day on the beach in the sun, a party or two maybe, but not Zuke, Chantal or Jacinta.

Jacinta! The frail, wide eyed and pale limbed Jacinta. He had to admit that he still felt a little guilty at what he had done. But then she hadn't exactly objected.

Inside the low house it was dark and cool. As his eyes became accustomed to the obscurity, he noted the traditional crucifix and gaudily painted picture of the Virgin and Child on the wall, the ornately framed photographs of grandparents and parents, and one of Jacinta in her first communion dress. There was a round table, a few chairs, a sideboard, little else.

Whispers were exchanged as Chantal shook the hand of a wiry old man who had worn his hat for so long that when he took it off he exposed an eggshell white dome of a head above a weather-beaten face.

It was he who led the way through the patio, a tiled area hung heavy with washing and crowded with potted plants. A small black mule stood tethered in a corner suffering the ceaseless humming of flies and eyeing the strangers who had come to look at the scene of the tragedy in its stable.

Two nights before Warren had made a ridiculous demand of the ouija, of the glass. He had challenged the supposed dead spirits it represented to deliver Jacinta to him, to make her come in all her virgin innocence to his room on the stroke of midnight, and both Zuke and Chantal had thought it hilarious.

They had all had quite a lot to drink. He had gone to bed and fallen asleep, content to have proved to his mad friends that all they were doing was playing with their own imagination.

Then the girl had actually come to his room. He had felt like a Victorian ogre deflowering a poor child prostitute, and it had not been that enjoyable because, throughout, he had been haunted by the conditions with which the ouija had countered his challenge. Jacinta would visit him, but if he took advantage of her he would be risking the unknown.

Absurd, but all the same unsettling. The next morning she could not be found, nor for the rest of the day and, that evening, when they had more soberly played the ouija again, they had been unnerved for the spirit supposedly communicating with them had insisted that it was Jacinta herself.

Now they were in her house, having been welcomed in by the grandparents.

The old man was pushing the stable door open, but turning his head, not wanting to look at what was inside.

3

Chantal started forward, but stepped back, covering her face with her hands. Zuke looked in, to pivot quickly round, gasping for breath. He went into the stable and stared with total disbelief at the horror confronting him. The frail Jacinta, in her black clothes and black rope-soled shoes, was hanging by the neck from a length of cord tied round a beam.

Her limp body rotated as the rope twisted and turned, showing now her head of fine glossy black hair, now the hideous contortions the facial muscles had suffered at the onset of death.

Her grey-green eyes, glazed, stared fixedly at the floor, seeing nothing; her once-pure white skin was now mottled, with patches of purple and mauve; her tongue, wet, brown and trickling blood, was swollen between clenched teeth.

Warren felt sick.

"Why are they leaving her there? Why don't they cut her down?" Zuke's voice was hardly audible, her expression incredulous.

"They're frightened," Chantal said, moving away. "They believed her to be a witch and don't want to touch her."

Warren looked around the stable. There was an assortment of implements and tools on a table. He picked up a rusty sickle; stood the stool, which she had kicked over, on its legs, got up on it and, closing his eyes, put his arm round the slim waist and gripped her as he sawed at the thick rope.

It gave. He dropped the sickle, held on to her tightly as he got down, then shuddered as her sickly mouth brushed his cheek, smearing it with blood and mucus.

Molest her and risk the unknown.

So the last few days on the Costa del Sol were ruined.

Peace of mind ceased to exist; he had to take sleeping pills recommended by a doctor, and when he awoke in the morning it was like going into a nightmare, not coming out of one.

He had come down, all on the firm's expense, to the Executive Toys and Games Fair being held at the new Hotel Don Enrique in Puerto Lucena.

It was a six-day event with all the familiar foreign reps and buyers drinking themselves into the ground while convincing each other that their products were more entertaining, more fulfilling and more profitable than those of their competitors.

It was fun and inevitably led to an encounter with some delectable stand hostess who would be impressed that at thirty-two he was not only a director of his company, but the innovator and creator of many of its successful games.

He had it made. It was an expression he had

used often enough about himself, finding that in the international world of hard sell, arrogance and self promotion were not a drawback, but an asset.

He had joined Swifts four years before, having been wooed away from the advertising agency which had handled the account. He'd been to art school because he was creative, followed by a spell in a publishing house as tea boy, then the move to a small agency where he had acquired enough knowledge to start the climb up the advertising ladder, till he had made it as Accounts Executive.

Swifts had hit a bad time and decided to advertise on television. He had advised against it, had suggested that they should think in terms of new products, new markets, and George Swift had offered him a directorship.

To go daily to an office near Windsor on an industrial estate had sounded mad, counter commuting, but it had been marvellous, leaving London in the morning on the M4 when everyone else was queueing to get in. It had been a valid reason to ask for a company car as well as a generous expense account, and after only three months he had come up with the idea for a series of board games for children which had proved a steady seller. The Farm Game, the Coal Mining Game, the Car Makers Game, the Chemists and Doctors Game. They were all more or less based on Monopoly, dice throwing, moving a symbol and winning or losing prestige.

The firm had done better, and then he had studied the adult market. He'd read countless books on the occult, had met a few nuts who believed in the darker powers of evil, eventually he had suggested a new game of cards with the fortune telling element of the Tarots, a modern design and a good advertising campaign behind it.

He'd found a talented artist, an attractive girl of twenty-two with whom he had had to work closely, their relationship had blossomed as had the game and they'd married when the game proved a best seller.

Then he'd topped it. An idea out of the blue, coming to him while driving home. Medium, a board game with accessories: a crystal ball, a little plastic talisman for each player, black magic symbols to move around. Pippa had designed it, Pippa his young wife, and it had gone into production straight away.

"You need a holiday, so I suggest you go down yourself and sell it at the exhibition," George Swift had said, "And stay on for a few days more."

"With Pippa?"

"Why not alone? You've been working together a lot, husbands and wives should occasionally be separated. Absence makes the heart grow fonder."

George was perceptive. His relationship with Pippa had become a little frayed lately with back biting and reproaches on petty issues. He had started making jokes about husbands and wives at the office, had started flirting with the secretaries again, and George had noticed.

"She's pregnant, you know," he'd told him.

"All the more reason for you to get away while you can, then. Once you're a dad you'll be stuck."

He had a room with a balcony overlooking the beach, and enjoyed the slower pace of life imposed by the Spanish character, even in the hotel ballroom packed as it was with some forty-five toy manufacturers' stands, and as many pretty girls.

On the first night he had turned the charm on an American hostess, who had turned the charm on him.

"My name is Warren Ryder, Stand 17, Swift's Board Games. England."

"Hi. I'm Zuke. Short for Zuleika would you believe?"

About twenty years old, maybe less, maybe more, she had freckles and gingery hair. Smart, efficient in a white pleated skirt and navy blue blazer, she'd flashed a smile of perfect teeth.

"You're the expert on the Tarots," she'd said, "Someone I know wants to meet you."

"Male or female?" he'd asked, working hard on the image he wanted to project.

She raised an eyebrow. "Female and French and a real medium."

From that moment on Zuke hadn't let him far out of her sight. She was by his side during the buffet lunch, at the Swift Stand whenever she could get away from her own, and as nine o'clock approached when the exhibition closed, she was back again, this time with an invitation.

"Chantal Daubigny, medium and spiritualist extraordinary, has invited us to dinner. I hope you don't have any other engagements."

She'd driven him there in her small car, skirting the tourist town to take a road leading up into the hills.

He hadn't had time to think about who he was going to meet, or why his hostess-to-be was so keen to have him as a guest, but when Zuke changed gear to negotiate a steep hairpin bend with a precipice on one side and a sheer rock wall on the other, he had started wondering just how far away this French woman lived.

"She was one of the first foreigners to buy up a ruin and convert it into something liveable," Zuke explained. "It was an olive mill. You'll be amazed by what she's done with it."

They'd reached the small Andalusian hamlet which was like a stage setting for *Carmen*; stark white houses with street lamps, the traditional balconies spilling over with hanging geraniums, but silent and deserted to the degree of being eerie.

"Is it inhabited?" he'd asked.

"Oh yes. But no one comes out before ten. Then you can hardly move for people. Right now they're probably all eating and watching television."

The occasional door and barred window was open and the familiar haunting blue light of the small screen confirmed what she'd said.

Zuke had slowed down to turn a corner, and the road was suddenly alive with goats, a whole herd of them trying to get by, tiny bells tinkling round their necks, their twisted horns butting the skinny rumps of those in front, squeezing by between the car and the whitewashed walls of the houses. Zuke drove on.

They passed the village square, the church, went down another steep cobbled street and stopped in front of a massive pair of wrought iron gates flanked by high walls.

"That's it. El Molino."

It had an air of wealth, the gate alone was a restored antique of quite beautiful symmetry.

"How old is this lady?" he'd asked.

"Probably older than she looks, but too young to be your mother."

And she wasn't at all what he'd expected. Chantal Daubigny came to open the gate herself, wearing a flowing dress of gossamer thin material. In her mid-forties, of medium height, swan-necked with long thick black hair, she had intense grey eyes and a quite beautiful mouth. Compared to Zuke she was delicate and moved like a ballet dancer. She studied him for a long time before saying anything, then opened the gate wide to let them in.

"You are much younger than I expected," she'd said.

"So are you."

She'd smiled acknowledging the compliment with a lowering of the eyes. She was very feminine.

"Please come in."

The interior of the house was quite astonishing. A marble tiled hallway led into a marble tiled drawing room furnished with low sofas and low occasional tables. The furnishings were in white, beige and brown, antiques blending with modern. There were art books on glass shelves, and oil paintings, drawings, and engravings were thoughtfully framed and artistically hung. Terrace windows gave out onto a patio and beyond a tropical garden surrounded a small swimming pool. In the distance were Puerto Lucena and the sea.

"I have been playing with your games. Swift's Tarots and Medium," she'd said. "You must be a very imaginative and talented young man to have devised such entertainment." She spoke clearly, slowly, her French accent adding a certain seductiveness to her appreciative comments.

She'd mixed them long cocktails which were ideally cool for the heat of the evening and they all sat back in the comfort of the sofas.

"For how long have you been studying the occult?"

"Not long," he'd answered, and explained that his interest in psychic matters was purely commercial, a means to an end.

"I have just purchased an exciting ouija table, late Victorian, English, carved with the letters of the alphabet round the circumference. I found it at the back of an antique shop in Seville. No one had any idea what it was. They in fact believed it to be some sort of sun dial. It's in the dining room."

They had exchanged the usual banalities, talked a little about themselves. He had told her about Pippa, their London life, their small one bedroomed flat situated conveniently in the centre where all the cinemas and theatres were within easy reach. Pippa was a film buff.

Then Jacinta had come in announcing that dinner was served. She was a waif of a girl, pale, and nervous. She wore a simple grey cotton dress with threadbare canvas shoes on her feet.

They had gone into the dining room, the oldest part of the house and once the heart of the olive mill. The old flag stones had been preserved and so had the beamed ceiling and the thick irregular undulating walls.

In the centre was a long refectory table on which four places had been laid with silver cutlery, crystal glasses, fine bone china plates and candles.

At the far end of the room was the ouija table with its gothic inlaid letters and numbers, a "oui" and a "non" on opposite sides.

"Did you know that the word ouija was derived from the French *oui* and the German *ja*?" Chantal had asked.

He had not.

And they had sat down to eat. He had wondered who the other guest was, only to realise that Jacinta was not a servant but a friend who occasionally came in to help.

After the meal, during which he had entertained them with stories of his days in advertising, avoiding the whole subject of the occult, Chantal had insisted that they should consult the ouija, and he had been polite and gone along with it.

The four of them had sat down round the table, a polished glass had been placed in the centre and all had dutifully put a finger tip on its upturned base.

"Nobody asks you to believe anything," Chantal had said. "Nobody makes any demands on you, but you will see, after a little while, you will believe. You will be made to believe."

The whole evening had been somewhat theatrical: candlelight, taped Bach on harpsichord, the full moon shining through the window, and Jacinta. The strange Jacinta.

"You have to be very polite," Chantal had said, and in a loftier tone addressing the ceiling, "Good evening, we have a new guest tonight. Mr. Warren Ryder."

The glass had started moving slowly and had spelt out W E L C O M E.

It had been one of them pushing it, obviously.

He'd looked at Chantal, who was concentrating, at Zuke who was staring at the table, at the young Spanish girl who had her eyes closed. She was, in a way, quite beautiful; her long hand poised delicately over the glass, her index finger pressing on the base. Yet there had been something ominous about her.

"What is your name?" Chantal had asked the ceiling.

VALDEZ.

"It's Armando Valdez Ortega. He always comes through when Jacinta is here," Chantal had explained. "He is her guide and guardian spirit and very accessible." Then she'd asked him, "Do you want to find out something special?"

"Not particularly," he'd replied.

"But you must ask a question," she'd insisted.

He'd thought it amusing at the time, had loved her enthusiasm, so had cleared his throat and had asked "Where is my wife?"

The glass had started to slide immediately.

SAINT STEPHENS.

"Saint Stephen's?" Chantal had been puzzled, "Does that mean anything to you?"

"There's a St. Stephen's Hospital," he'd said, "quite near us, where she's been recently for ante-natal consultations. But I don't think she'd be there right now."

"Then ask again, we must get a clear answer."

"Where is Phillipa, my wife, right now, tonight?"

The goblet had not moved, yet somehow he'd sensed that it had hesitated. His imagination. Tricks his hostess had played.

Then the glass had glided to two numbers, the "3" and the "4," and had started spelling out his street.

"My home address," he'd said.

"Ask why it first mentioned Saint Stephen's? Was it the past?"

The glass had moved quickly, so quickly that he could hardly believe it, across the shiny marble to the "non" on his right.

"Was it the future then?" Chantal asked.

"Oui." The glass spun across the centre of the table, with no hesitation this time, as though an electrical force had propelled it.

Then, quite spontaneously, feeling that he was in contact with an unexplainable source of knowledge, he had asked, "She is going to St. Stephen's in the future?"

"Oui."

"For the baby?" At the back of his mind he had wanted to ask whether it would be a boy or a girl.

A C C I D E N T.

He had looked at Zuke, at Chantal, at Jacinta, but they had just stared at the table.

"An accident, when?" he'd ventured.

S O O N.

And he had felt a little sick because the next question that had crossed his mind had been incredibly selfish. "Will I have to go back?"

But the actual phrase had not formed itself

immediately, a rapid succession of thoughts had flashed through his mind—Phillipa in hospital with a miscarriage, an early return from his holiday, back to her in bed with tubes in her veins, in a wheelchair, the baby dead, her dead, an unexpected freedom for him.

He hadn't asked the question. He hadn't mouthed the phrase, had not uttered a sound, but the glass unprompted had started moving and had spelt out F R E E D O M.

Unnerved, he had pushed his chair back and got up and broken the spell of whatever it was.

"I don't understand," he'd said. "I don't understand how it could have read my mind."

"It did not read your mind, *mon cher*," Chantal had explained. "You are reading your own mind. The ouija is quite understandable if you simply accept that, as human beings, we do not know the full extent of our capabilities. We are sending out and receiving subconscious thoughts to and from each other continually. The ouija arrests these thoughts for us by means of our own electrical impulses. We are not necessarily in the presence of demons or spirits or the devil or ghosts here, what we might be doing is psychoanalysing ourselves by means of telepathy. If we're not, then we must be in contact with the dead. There can be no other explanation."

"But how would I know that my wife is going to have an accident?"

"You don't know that, but either the dead do, or else it is wishful thinking. If you are honest with yourself you will admit that you have, on occasions, thought that if your wife had an accident and was incapacitated for a while you would be free to do . . . what you wish? You are away from her for the moment, you have been tempted by something young and refreshing, and your subconscious mind is doing the rest. Or not?"

He had thought the explanation typically French, and probably unpleasantly close to the truth. He certainly preferred to believe in his own wishful thinking being transmitted to the glass, than it being a message from some spirit.

"Perhaps there are certain vibrations going on between yourself and Zuke, or Jacinta, of which you are unaware," Chantal had gone on, "and you went through the process of rejecting such ideas because you are married? Then an accident came to mind, to which you added St. Stephen's because that is where she is to have the baby?"

"Maybe," he had said, and smiled through a sigh at Zuke.

Zuke had driven him back down the hill to his hotel after that and he had naturally asked her up to his room for a nightcap.

There had been the usual hesitation, what he imagined as the female need to be persuaded, and he had let it go, unsettled by the evening's developments.

For the following three nights, till the last day of the fair, he had gone back up to Chantal's with Zuke, eating and drinking and playing the ouija, sometimes with Jacinta, sometimes not.

Then on the fourth morning he had been woken up by a knock on the door, a discreet tap in case he was asleep, hardly audible. The cleaners, he had presumed.

On opening the door he had been surprised to see Jacinta. She looked straight at him, her green eyes searching his face, it seemed, for an expression, a sign, which clearly wasn't there, for she quickly looked down, shyly, and had nervously said, "Doña Chantal would like to see you. It is important."

She was wearing black, a sleeveless blouse, a skirt, flat rope-soled shoes with laces crisscrossed up her ankles.

"Come in," he'd suggested. "I've nothing to offer you but duty free whisky in a tooth mug, but come in."

"Just water," she'd said, slipping into the room.

"Sit down."

There were the deck chairs on the balcony,

the unmade bed, or a straight backed chair next to the dresser.

She'd chosen the chair, sat on her hands, her feet and knees together.

"Is something wrong that it's so urgent?"

She'd shrugged her shoulders, shaken her head, studied him in his bathrobe, glancing apprehensively at the bed.

His imagination?

She had come to his room, slim, little, pale and vulnerable, maybe a gift from Chantal, or more likely a taunt.

He'd gone to the bathroom and rinsed out the glass, and had been surprised to see her standing in the doorway when he turned. She had smiled at him wiping the glass with one of the towels. He'd filled it with water, handed it to her and watched her drink it down in a few thirsty gulps.

He'd wanted to touch the smoothness of her long neck, reach behind her ears to feel the back of her head under the mass of jet black hair.

She'd put the glass down on the washbasin and pointed to a line of ants that had found something sweet on the floor, biscuit crumbs from the night before, a whole army of reddish ants.

Suddenly she had stamped on them rather unpleasantly with a peasant indifference that was disconcertingly violent. Jacinta had then turned round, opened the door and gone out into the corridor with a nodding thanks. It was as though she had suddenly realised that she was in the very type of danger she wanted to be in but could not go through with it.

"Doña Chantal would like to see you. It is urgent." He had got his marching orders.

He'd found Zuke sitting on the front patio steps.

"Did that Jacinta summon you as well?" she'd asked.

"Yes."

"Well she's not here. Neither of them are."

Warren had sat down next to her in the shade and looked round the front garden.

It had been carefully laid out and was tended with love and care: the bougainvillaea, the cyclamens, the climbing roses all carefully trained up the side of the house, on the inside of the surrounding wall. There was a jacaranda tree, pruned olive trees, mimosa, banana trees with their flat floppy leaves. He would have liked a few weeds here and there, a little wilderness, but Chantal was a tidy, meticulous person.

"That girl Jacinta gives me the creeps," Zuke had said, about nothing, and he had not commented. He'd felt he had the choice of both, and the Spanish waif was somehow a more tantalising proposition. A challenge in a way.

Then Chantal had turned up in her Renault. "You have come just at the right moment," she'd shouted, "You can help me with this!"

In the back of the car was a marble table, wrapped in a plastic sheet.

"Is this the urgency?" Zuke had asked.

"What urgency?"

"We were both asked to come here urgently, by your faithful messenger and servant."

"Jacinta? No! I haven't even seen her this morning."

Chantal had been too excited at getting the table into the house to make any more of it, but Zuke had not liked getting orders without knowing why.

"I'm not lifting a finger to help, let alone lifting a heavy chunk of marble, till I know why we're here."

"I don't know why you're here."

"Is Jacinta around?"

"I told you, I haven't seen her this morning. Maybe she'll turn up."

"Did she know you were collecting the table this morning?" he'd asked.

"Possibly."

"Then she must have decided we'd be needed," Zuke had said. "She certainly couldn't help you without snapping in two herself."

"Don't be bitchy, Zuke," Chantal had protested, "Jacinta is nearly like a daughter to me."

"Nearly is the key word, Señora. No mother of mine would get me to slave away like you get her to do."

"She is well rewarded."

They had got the table top out of the car and had carried it up the garden path. By the time they had got it into the living room, together with the pedestal base, they had all been too exhausted to care about anything but sitting down.

"When I've got my breath back," Chantal puffed, "I will get you a nice long drink. We could have a swim also, and then perhaps try out the table?"

She had then told them that she had commissioned it from a stone mason in Malaga a year or so back, before she had found the antique board, and that she had also had an alabaster goblet made, mounted on castors to roll over it in imitation of the original Victorian ouija games.

Chantal had then suggested that both he and Zuke should stay the night, in separate guest rooms, which is what had prompted him to jokingly ask the ouija to send him the virgin Jacinta.

Molest her and risk the unknown.

She had come to his room, timid, silent, like a human sacrifice to some tyrant god, and because he had eaten well and drunk too much, he had acted out the fantasy, undressed her, stood nude and resplendent in front of her, had picked her up and laid her on the bed and undone her. The shock had been her virginity. He had never expected that.

And the next day she had gone missing, her grandparents, concerned, had called at the house to see if she was there and later, worried because there had been no sign of her, Chantal had begged Zuke and himself to help her consult the ouija.

Warren had complyingly placed his finger on the new alabaster goblet with Zuke, and Chantal had asked if anyone was there.

The goblet had moved to the Yes.

"Who are we in contact with?"

And the goblet had moved slowly back to the centre of the table, then inched its way to the "J," cut across the top of the circle to the "A," slid three letters to the "C," along the edge to the "I," gathered momentum to the "N," skated freely to the "T" and ended up at the "A" again.

"Jacinta?"

"That's because we've all been thinking of her," Zuke had said.

"You are Jacinta?" Chantal had asked.

YES. Straight there, no hesitation.

"We are speaking to the spirit of Jacinta?"

YES.

"Does that mean that you are dead?"

And Warren had felt that the power had been cut off, had felt that the impulses had gone.

CHAPTER TWO

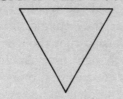

A NEIGHBOUR of the grandparents came into the stable with a white bed sheet and helped him wrap up the stiffening body.

Warren was in control of himself now, able to look at her face, able to loosen the rope around her neck and wipe off some of her blood from his shirt sleeve.

They carried her out into the patio and through to the house where they laid her down on the floor. The door was crowded with the curious now, the "vecinos," some crying, some crossing themselves, some just staring at the horror.

Chantal nodded encouragingly at him, Zuke

gave him a brave smile, and then they left, duty done.

The three of them stuck together like criminals from then on. They returned to Chantal's villa and discussed the whole tragic business endlessly: what they should say, what they should not say, what they thought they should do, what they thought they should not do.

Chantal saw the position more clearly than he did. Having known Jacinta over two years she felt that the girl's suicide had absolutely nothing to do with any of them as far as the authorities were concerned. They were not in England, nor France nor America, there would not be an in-depth enquiry into what she had been doing before she took her life, there would be no follow up.

The people in Jacinta's street and her family were not surprised. Her case history was so simple that her death was not a shock. She had been brought up by her grandparents, her mother having died giving her birth and her father drowning at sea shortly afterwards. She had been a good Catholic, had gone to church more regularly than many children, but from the age of sixteen had started to talk of visions and bad dreams and had become a source of concern. When Chantal had befriended her and employed her on occasions, it had been a great relief, and the money she had brought in had been gratefully accepted. She had never seen a doctor, let alone a psychiatrist.

"We are over-reacting to the whole thing, you see," Chantal explained. "The local people are accepting the event at face value. Suicides are not uncommon in any country, and it is understood that for some of us life becomes unbearable. She decided she had had enough. Her choice."

"But supposing it wasn't a choice?" Zuke voiced.

"Meaning what?"

"Meaning that we're all trying to avoid talking about the coincidence of the ouija's warning."

"If we even consider that," Warren said, "Then we're admitting that we believe in its powers."

"I admit it," Chantal said.

"So do I," Zuke agreed.

And looking at them, he realised that however much he enjoyed their company, however much he would love to stay, it was time he broke away from them, time to sever the relationship, before it was too late.

The next morning he was woken up at eight by a loud knock on his hotel bedroom door.

His first thought was that it would be Chantal, then Zuke, or both, insisting on accompanying him to the airport, which he didn't want.

But it was neither. It was Jacinta's grandfather holding out a badly wrapped paper packet done up with green string.

He took it, weighed it in his hand. It felt like a book. He thanked the man and watched him walk away.

He closed the door, removed the string, ripped open the poor quality paper and stared at what looked like the front section of an old reference book. There was the front cover of well-weathered brown leather, all the preface pages numbered in Roman figures, and the first hundred and twenty pages of actual text.

The book was entitled *A Discourse on the Reality of the Occult*. It was a translation from the Spanish, dated 1982 and the original author's name was Armando Valdez Ortega.

He flipped the pages over quickly, then started again turning them over one by one expecting to find a relevant passage, a cross against another warning perhaps, a message of sorts.

There was nothing. Half a book. Why? Was it a way in which Jacinta's relations were letting him know that they suspected him of being the cause of her death, accusing him of sorcery, of witchcraft, of practising the black arts?

Whatever it was, it triggered off a feeling of great insecurity and a more pressing desire to get the hell out of the area, to get out of the country and back to the safety of London.

He got down to the packing, deciding to leave straight away, wait for hours at Malaga airport maybe, but leave the hotel where people obviously knew he could be reached.

What a disastrous end to a break which had started with such promise.

And he would miss Zuke.

Between her and Chantal they had hit a number of delicate nails fairly and squarely on the head. Last night, after driving him back down from Chantal's, he and Zuke had sat at a terrace café for a goodbye drink. He'd ordered a white wine, Zuke had asked for a Coke. No alcoholic bravado. That is what she wanted, she was not a schoolgirl trying to impress.

"How old are you?" he'd asked.

"That's not a gentlemanly question. Twenty-one."

"Why did you come here?"

She'd told him, without much enthusiasm. A series of adventures had got her here; she was looking for something, didn't know what it was and hadn't found it yet. That sort of life.

"Like you, I'm a lost soul," she'd said.

"I'm a lost soul?" He'd been surprised. "What makes you say that?"

"Observation. It's in the eyes, the hangdog look. It's the first time you've been away from home in years, isn't it?"

"I suppose so."

"There you are. Holidays with parents, holidays with your wife, then suddenly, zap! You're alone and you discover yourself. What you discover is that you don't know yourself at all as a one man person. You discover what it's like to wash alone, brush your teeth alone, pee alone, dress alone. Though you may have thought you always did these things by yourself, you realise that there was always someone else hanging around, often waiting for you to finish. Eating alone, Jesus, that's an experience, don't you think?"

He had thought of it. He had eaten two lunches by himself and hated it so much that he found himself ready to talk to anyone.

"What's it been like alone in bed—apart from the one fateful night?"

Had he imagined a reproachful tone, a tinge of jealousy? "Comfortable," he'd replied.

"Is your wife fat then?"

"No."

"You like stretching. I can see you. Spread-eagled on your back, with just a sheet over you in case someone bursts into the room in the middle of the night and finds you naked."

He'd smiled, laughed. It was a disconcertingly true insight into his character.

"Am I right? Tell me I'm right. You haven't been able to sleep completely naked just on top of the mattress?"

"I'm frightened of mosquitos," he'd said.

"Biting your little dick?"

Intimate, personal, amusing.

"I was thinking of going to bed with you tonight," she'd then said, "but I've decided against it."

"What put you off?"

"Jacinta."

"What I did?"

"Not what you did."

"The fact that I did it at all?"

"No, not that either. You shouldn't feel so guilty on that score. It's that somehow I think that you were the one that was used."

"How?"

"I don't know how. But I feel that you, Chantal and I are somehow being played as some kind of pawns in a ouija game we can't understand."

"Then it's time this pawn left the board," he'd said.

"But you can't do that. You didn't place yourself on the board, you were put there."

"By whom?"

"Whoever or whatever motivated Jacinta to kill herself."

It had sent a shiver down his back. "You're talking in riddles."

"No, I'm not. You know what I'm talking about, at least you know as much as I do what I'm talking about. I think we're caught up in something we can't stop."

"Black magic?" he'd suggested, jokingly.

"It's a pretty banal label, but good enough for the moment. I feel the three of us are involved in something which we won't be able to control unless we're very careful, and instinct tells me that the three of us should not separate and that if we do, if we try to run away, or attempt to forget what happened like a bad dream, nasty things will happen."

"What should I do then?"

"Just make sure you don't abandon us completely. Write to us, come back. Come back as soon as you can."

He'd finished his wine, she'd finished her Coke, he'd paid the waiter and they had sauntered back up the road toward the hotel where they'd briefly kissed and said goodbye.

For the third night running he'd taken a sleeping pill, and now he was packing.

It took his mind from thinking, the settling of the hotel account, the whole business of winding up the trip. On the spur of the moment he wrapped up the half book and addressed it to Chantal with a note of thanks for everything.

He didn't want it, didn't want to have anything that reminded him of Jacinta and the whole horrific episode.

He got one of the hotel porters to deliver it, then went to the bar and toyed with a drink till his taxi arrived to collect him.

The driver put his suitcase in the boot, opened the door for him and he settled back on the hot leather seat to relax and enjoy the last looks at the Mediterranean coastline.

But an anxiety was clouding everything. Was it guilt at leaving the way he was leaving, escaping, running away? Guilt at not having taken the book? Or was it quite simply the guilt of having been unfaithful to Pippa, both physically and mentally?

He was admitting it, wasn't he? Zuke's liveliness compared to Pippa's. Her quick thinking, her humour had impressed him, and Chantal's house had been an enchantment.

Her way of life in the sun had made him discontented with his own lot. Her environment, that spacious living room with all the paintings, the books, the tiles, the antiques, the garden and its swimming pool all added up to one very simple thing. Single living, one person doing what they wanted to do without having to consult or argue or compromise.

He would be going back to the ever-dusty sitting room with its thousand plants, the bedroom with its worn carpet, the fitted cupboards with the doors that didn't close, Pippa's study, her den, which was the untidiest place on earth and the kitchen which was also her province, though he seemed to do most of the cooking.

His world was the chair in front of the television, his dressing room, and his office in Windsor which was continually invaded by everyone.

So what was there to look forward to? Pippa's companionship, her love and her interest in all he did, and more important, the baby to come. Fatherhood, whatever that entailed. It was still far off, a whole seven months, nothing showing yet, but it was exciting, an excitement he had never experienced before. Other than that, George would take him out for the inevitable pub lunch to bring him up to date on all the disasters that had happened while he was away, and he'd get back in the saddle, which he enjoyed, and which was safe. At least he had got quite a few foreign orders from the Fair.

Jacinta, Zuke and Chantal would have to remain a secret with him, that was all. He might mention them in passing to Pippa, but it would be wiser to say as little as possible. Pippa was an innocent, she would not jump to the obvious conclusions on hearing that he had spent his free time with three females, but others might and it was all avoidable.

The taxi drew up outside international departures. A porter took his suitcase to the check in; he went to passport control, to customs, to the departure lounge where he waited flicking through a magazine.

The flight number was called, echoed out in two languages, he queued to get onto the hot tarmac, then walked in the heat, up the steps into the air conditioned humming airliner. There was a little push, a little ungentlemanliness to get a window seat which was essential for the last holiday enjoyment.

The engine revved and shuddered, they took off and he made the usual deliberate effort to think of other things than the possible accident.

For a moment he imagined Jacinta sitting next to him, a messenger of death, cold, white, blood trickling from her mouth. It was silly.

He forced himself to think out the details of a new game he had had at the back of his mind before leaving: Theatres. It would give him a chance to visit the West End, get a few cheaper tickets to first nights or previews perhaps.

Pippa would like that. A rival company's Film-maker had done well. Maybe he would call it Impresario: each player would be a producer of classical drama, opera, ballet, musicals or pop concerts, the educational content would be high with Shakespeare's works on the cards, and George always liked the idea of high educational content.

Lunch was now on its way, the distribution of convenience foods on convenient throw away plastic trays.

Maybe the games should be printed on plastic? Plastic dishes were thrown away, but plastic games were preserved. Something for Market Research to look into. What materials did people who played board games like best?

One of the hostesses reminded him of Jacinta. He wouldn't be rid of her memory that easily. Why had she hung herself? Why the book?

The hostess walked down the aisle from the pilot's cabin a little more briskly than was usual and spoke to her colleagues. It was nothing very exceptional, but there was a tenseness in the walk, in the gestures, that unsettled him. They stopped moving the trolleys, they stopped serving, and asked for his tray back before he could start eating.

Had they served the wrong food? Was there a food poison scare?

The *fasten your seat belts/no smoking* sign flashed on, a bell sounded and a male voice came through. The Captain, cool, calm, trained to be so. Owing to a minor defect in the fuel system they would be landing in Madrid within ten minutes. There was no cause for alarm, they apologised for any inconvenience caused and everyone would be informed immediately of any alteration in flight plans. They started the descent.

He'd flown enough times to wonder why it hadn't happened before. There seemed to be no cause for panic, a few of the older Spanish ladies took out their fans and fanned themselves nervously, muzak was piped through to keep the atmosphere jolly, he found himself pleased to have a magazine to look at.

There was an article on babies—well that of course would be the answer to all the problems, it would change the pattern of their lives and they would now have an excuse to move out to the country.

He had had enough of the London life which was getting ridiculously expensive.

There would be the search for a house, an open plan kitchen-living room, a nursery, a garden with a swing and a slide, all that. Most of his contemporaries were fathers, he'd probably be pleased to have something in common with some of the friends he'd lost.

They landed in Madrid without mishap and taxied close enough to the airport buildings for him to presume that it would be a long delay, maybe a change of plane.

They were asked to file out and were put in a holding lounge. Some people were agitated, others less so. He was not one to obey the shepherd's orders without question, so he asked one of the hostesses what was happening. It would either be a matter of waiting for the plane to be checked, or for a flight from Gatwick to come and take them.

"Two, three hours?" he suggested.

"At least," she said.

He decided to telephone Pippa to stop her from coming to meet him. She would not have left home yet.

He found a phone booth, had enough pesetas because he was a sufficiently seasoned traveller to know never to travel without the necessary coins for emergency calls, for newspapers, sweets, tips. He dialled, waited patiently. Eleven o'clock on Sunday morning in London, she might still be in bed, or tidying up furiously so that the house would look all beautiful on his arrival.

She answered, surprised, then concerned. Was he all right? Was anything wrong? He explained that he was stuck in Madrid, probably for three or four hours, maybe more. She was disappointed, but relieved that it was nothing more. Not to worry, she would check with Gatwick on his arrival time and would still meet him. He said it would be wiser for him to ring on his arrival at the airport, that would be the best way, in case she was given wrong information, which had happened before. She said OK, said that she loved him, which was nice, and he rang off.

He glanced at himself in a boutique mirror and caught the reflection of a girl passing by. The eyes were familiar, the long hair, the timid smile. Jacinta again. He turned abruptly. There wasn't even anyone there.

He walked about looking everywhere at everything. He checked the departures board. Heathrow 12:30. No gate yet announced.

He went to the airline's check in, explained his situation. He couldn't bear the idea of waiting if he didn't have to. Only a simple one-way. It could be arranged. He might have to pay extra but it would be re-imbursed. He liked playing games, of course, he was in the games business, beating the clock, beating the system. They swiftly gave him a new ticket, checked his passport, his luggage would be sent on. He was in through the gate on the last call, leaving the others behind to wait for hours. He would be in London half an hour before he had originally planned, with the elimination of the Gatwick journey.

The comfort now of the smaller, cosier plane. Different air hostesses, no Jacinta here, British comfort, British security. No problems, no one else had been as quick off the mark as he had and that made him feel really good.

The holiday, the sun, the beach had after all done him good. He was full of vigour and vim and it wouldn't be that bad going back to work.

He had a good lunch with wine, and a cloudless sky all the way. France was below, then the sea, then the South Coast and eventually they came down low over London in bright sunlight. He could see Windsor Castle, clear, the winding silver Thames, the neatness. He could nearly smell the fresh mown grass lawns, nearly hear the thudding of the cricket bats in the village games. There was a lot going for him.

He saw tarmac, Heathrow, clean cars, shining solid chrome, the row of black taxis. Why not? Why not end the holiday in style? Ten pounds, twelve, fifteen? He didn't care.

To surprise Pippa, maybe having a bath, getting lunch. He'd take her to a restaurant, if she hadn't eaten. Tonight they'd go out anyway.

The M4. So familiar, so nice to get back to. Hammersmith Flyover, Earls Court, the Cromwell Road, Gloucester Road ahead, left into

Cornwall Gardens with all its trees and foliage and shade on a hot summer's day.

The taxi drew up, he got out, paid. He inserted the familiar key, not used for ten days, in the front door and the familiar smell he'd forgotten, a mixture of wax polish and newly laid carpet recently put down by the landlord at the tenants' great expense. He went up the first flight of stairs, to his own door. Flat One. Should he ring? Surprise her and just walk in?

He didn't enjoy giving shocks, so he rang the bell, his own bell, usually heard from within. How often had he rung it himself, once? Maybe twice when they had first moved in as newlyweds two years ago and only had one key between them.

The door opened.

Pippa was in her towelling wrap, a little make up, very beautiful, tanned, her hair dishevelled as though she had been running. She looked at him with such astonishment, that it was as though she didn't recognise him.

"I caught a flight to London from Madrid."

She couldn't stop him coming in, but he felt that that was what she was trying to do, as though he were a stranger who should not be there, an intruder. He leaned over to give her a kiss, and was surprised to taste wine on her lips. Her breath smelt of wine.

Then he heard a sound coming from the bedroom, a familiar sound, the springs of the bed taking the strain of pressure, of weight, of someone getting out of bed and, not thinking, his mind not working nearly quickly enough, he walked down the short hallway and went into the bedroom and saw the man's naked back. The bed was not just unmade but in chaos, the bolster on the floor, pillows in the middle of the mattress, clothes everywhere.

The man turned round, apologetic. It was George.

The anxiety welled up. Was that what it had been all the time, a deeply imbedded suspicion, something he had not been able to work out?

His mind worked very fast now. All the pieces of the past suddenly slotted into a pattern. George's insistence that he should go for a holiday, the firm paying, George's holiday last year coinciding with Pippa being away in Edinburgh. The Toy Fair in Torquay, the night of the ball, George and Pippa disappearing, himself with George's wife, not knowing.

He turned round. She was behind him, covering herself, covering her nudity, her feet together, her toes painted, trembling a little.

Was it a fear of violence, or a fear of hurting him, of upsetting him, for there was love between them, there must still be love and affection?

He was going to ask George how long it had been going on, ask Pippa, but that was senseless, they would lie, or they would tell the truth and he would not know what to believe.

There was so much at stake, so much of the future, so much of the past at stake, everything was put in danger by this one encounter and he knew it would be best to leave, just leave, walk out, run away from it to think. He had to give himself time, give them time. He had to act normally, intelligently. He turned, faced her.

She hadn't moved, she was frightened, every one of his thoughts had gone through her mind as well.

"The real tragedy of this," he said in a very clear, very steady voice, "Is that I will never really be certain whose child it is."

An expression of horror came into her own eyes and she was unable to speak.

And he left, walked down the stairs, through the front door and out into the street.

He started running, running fast, for fear of her stepping out on the balcony and shouting after him, of begging him to come back, begging for a chance to justify, to explain.

At the corner of the gardens he stopped, paused for breath, aware that people he had passed had stared at him curiously, a man running so fast was not that usual.

He walked on, slowly now.

He didn't want to see people, he wanted only to get away, far away from everything he knew, far away enough to think things out. He wanted to sit down in some long grass by a river, he wanted to sit down on a beach and look at the sea, but he was in the heart of London where it was impossible to escape.

What to do? What to do? Whom to consult? Chantal? Zuke? The ouija?

The ouija? Could it be of its doing? The warning came to him again too clearly. *Molest her and risk the unknown.* The glass had predicted tragedy even before he had spent that night with Jacinta.

He was going mad. Whether he liked to admit it or not, the damned ouija was having an effect. He kept thinking about it, could not shake its haunting. He was perturbed.

He turned on his heels and made his way back to the flat. It was senseless to try and ignore what had happened, senseless to dramatise his part in it. Self pity would not help either. He would face both of them, demand an explanation, sort it out one way or another.

A car came towards him, stopped. The driver got out.

It was George, in a shirt and trousers, with bare feet, in a terrible state of agitation.

"Have you seen her?"

"Pippa? No."

"We've got to find her. She ran out of the house, quite hysterical."

"Looking for me?"

"No. She mentioned a friend, someone around here I suppose. She was just in her bathrobe."

"Did she mention a name?"

"Yes. Jacinta, I think. I saw her going this way, towards the tube station."

They got into the car, George crashed the gears, put his foot flat down, narrowly missing a pedestrian, going through the lights at the Cromwell Road junction, braking abruptly outside the underground.

For an older man he was quick: out of the car and down the steep stairs, people turning to look at him.

Warren was at the top of the last flight and saw it all happen. The silver grey train coming in at speed, Pippa's slight figure naked under the bathrobe, people gasping, Pippa taking off, the bathrobe like wings flapping and the bird being smashed against the flat glass window of the driver's cabin. The screech of brakes, the screams, the howls. George down there reaching out for her, smacked away by the impact of the train, reeling back to fall on the platform, while she slid down between the bumpers and was drawn under the wheels to be crushed, dismembered, then incinerated by the live rail.

Alarm, chaos, people everywhere, in all directions.

He moved through the crowd as though in a nightmare. George was hurt, bones broken, lying there on the platform in agony. The train rumbled backwards, the crowd pressed forward, he saw little of her, but enough, a butcher's carcass wrapped in the charred bathrobe.

The police were there now, with firemen, ambulance men, asking questions.

"Suicide was it?"

"Oh yes. Quite deliberate. Fellow with her tried to save her, got hit back onto the platform."

"Where are you taking her?" One official voice asked another.

"St. Stephen's."

"Move along there, please, sir."

"I'm her husband."

"Your wife was it?"

"Yes."

His wife . . . his child . . . an accident . . . As predicted.

CHAPTER THREE

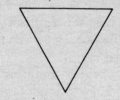

ZUKE awoke with an unexplainable feeling of loss. It was a sensation she had never experienced before.

She got up, made herself a cup of coffee, got back into bed and stared at her reflection in the mirror.

She was a mess. Her hair was awful and her tan was fading, giving her face a yellowish pallor. In the last few days she had let herself go too far and she would have to pull herself together.

The trouble was that there was nothing to look forward to. The toy fair had been a chance freelance job, and now there was nothing to do except think, which was just what she wanted to avoid.

She had no friends, either. Not any that she wanted to see. Chantal would only talk about Jacinta and insist on consulting the ouija again, and Warren, whom she really rather liked, was now with his wife back in London, probably never to be seen again.

Then there was the emptiness in her stomach which she knew was not hunger, but fear. Fear on two counts.

Count one was fantasy. They had dabbled in the occult and had disturbed something unfathomable resulting in Jacinta's death.

Count two was reality. She had lost out to that same Jacinta, Warren preferring to take her to bed, though she was thin, definitely unsophisticated and younger.

Christ, it wasn't that Warren was that marvellous a man, but he had been fun. Cheeky was an apt English word, cheeky looking, cheeky in manner. The very way he had challenged the ouija, dared it to send him the "Virgin Jacinta," as he had called her. The man *she* had lost her virginity to had never been as excited by the prospect.

The bell rang and she quickly slipped on her knee length T-shirt and went to open the apartment door.

In the corridor stood a youth she had never

seen before. He was holding out something
solid wrapped in cheap brown paper and tied
with green string.

"¿Señorita Zuleika?"

"Sí?"

"Para ti. De mi prima."

"Gracias."

Whom did she know who had a generous
cousin? As he left she noticed he was wearing
a black arm band. She closed the door, undid
the thin green string, unwrapped the paper and
stared at the half book in her hands. It had old
print, there were some hundred faded pages of
what seemed to be an English textbook. The
title at the top of each page was unsettling—*A
Discourse on the Reality of the Occult.*

She flipped through it hoping for some en-
lightenment, a card telling her who it was from
perhaps, but all she found was a paragraph
boxed in by wavy inky lines on one of the middle pages. It started with a quote, apparently
from Marlowe's Faust.

Ah, Pythagoras metempsycossis [sic] were
that true. This soule should flie from me,
and I be changed into some brutish beast

And it was followed by a comment by the unknown author.

Metempsychosis therefore is no new thought. The transmigration of the soul, the passage of the soul of a human being after death into a new body was a tenet of the Pythagorians and certain Eastern religions, especially Buddhism. When the character, Jacinta, in the novel which caused my igno-miny, hung herself and thereafter transmi-grated her soul into that of a friend, I was not putting forward a new theory, but sim-ply expounding an old one.

I was not putting forward a new theory? Who was the *I*? Who was the author? She went through the book again, page by page, realised that she had only the middle section, then found a clue to the author's identity in a trans-lator's note to the reader.

Ortega chooses to use the word "anima" for soul, not "alma" or "espiritu," suggesting "soul from purgatory."

Ortega. Valdez Ortega, the spirit with whom they had been communicating through the ouija?
She closed the book, put it gently down on a chair and moved to the window. Jacinta's cousin had delivered the book. It was going to go on. The haunting. One way or another, if

she stayed here, it would go on. Jacinta's family, her friends, her acquaintances would be watching her, a connection had been made locally between her and the girl's death and she was not going to be allowed to forget it.

She didn't question why the book had been delivered, nor on whose orders. Someone was motivating people to involve her further in the aftermath of the tragedy.

Someone or something. And she now felt it very necessary to get away.

She went to her cupboard and took her canvas hold-all down from the top shelf. She opened it and stuffed a few essential clothes in it, spare shoes, her make up, her valuables. She got dressed, in her cut-off jeans, a T-shirt and sandals, got her passport, her money, paper and pen, wrote a note to the landlord and another to Chantal, and without a backward glance, without giving herself time for a second thought, she left the apartment, the block, headed down the street for the main road and walked east, not wanting to wait for a bus, not wanting to stand still, not wanting to give anything a chance to catch up with her.

Three days ago she had had to return the car hired by the toy manufacturers she had represented, so now it was public transport or hitch hiking.

She didn't care. She walked. She headed for

Almeria, then maybe would go North to Alicante, Valencia, Barcelona, maybe even France.

It didn't matter. She walked. She walked for
an hour or so till she was well away from the
town, and then sat down on her hold-all and,
in hippy autostop tradition, thumbed every
passing vehicle.

An articulated lorry came over the hilltop
and she stood up and thumbed away like mad.
There were three men in the front, the middle
one a remarkably angelic looking boy with
blond curls. They grinned at her, waved, but
didn't stop.

She walked on slowly, thankful that she was
only wearing the minimum of clothing, thankful also for the shade afforded by a line of pine
trees.

There was a sound in the distance. She was
on top of a hill now and could look back down
along the snake-like road whence she had
come. A saloon car, white, one of those stan-
dard models made in Spain, newer, better than
most, appeared, a driver in front, a lady in the
back. The car passed smoothly, quietly, the
woman was young, very young, a girl of her
own age, dark hair, dressed in white. She had
the profile of . . . well, she had the profile of
Jacinta if she cared to admit it, quite beautiful,
but aristocratic. To her surprise the car stopped

some distance ahead and the man got out and beckoned to her.

She walked faster, got to the car, out of breath.

"¿*Dónde va*? To where are you going?" He spoke with a pleasant lilting accent. A nice looking man, middle aged, heavy set, glasses, amiable.

"Valencia," she said.

She had learnt never to answer back in Spanish if addressed in English. Everyone loved to speak a foreign language, loved to practise it, that is why some of them stopped and gave you lifts.

"Get in, get in," he urged.

She got into the front seat next to him, then turned to greet the woman.

There was no one in the back.

That was strange, for she had definitely seen a girl sitting in the back, behind the driver, black hair, white dress, young with a profile like . . . Jacinta.

"Are you all right? Please, your seat belt."

He helped her with it, in that he handed her the clip and did not stretch across her, a sensuous movement that a less considerate man might have attempted straight away.

"Are you all right?"

"Yes. Yes, fine thank you," she said. "I just

had the impression you had someone in the back."

"Oh, are you afraid of driving with me alone?"

"No. Not at all."

She wanted to reassure him. He was far too nice a man for her to make him feel uncomfortable.

He smiled at her as he put the car into gear, he checked the rear view mirror, checked out of the window. He was a careful driver, a family man with a million responsibilities.

For a Spaniard he was tall, heavy set, with muscular shoulders, a good head of hair, neatly turned out and certainly not mean with the aftershave. What she found disconcerting was the small panel of photographs above the ashtray, an imitation gold frame enclosing four snaps of his children with a cross motif and a St. Christopher medallion. He didn't have a doll hanging from the back window, or lace curtains, as some did, but he was getting pretty near the mark. His house would be full of plastic trinkets and holiday souvenirs.

"From where are you?" he asked.

"Originally I'm from Arizona."

"And you are a student tourist?"

"That's it, yes."

"How long have you been in Spain?"

"About a year."

She told him briefly what she was at, didn't go into great details about her background, but just gave him the impression that she was a girl whom he might be quite proud to introduce to his family. Her father, she lied, was a professor at Harvard who liked her to travel the world and learn the ways of others.

They talked of the dangers of the road, the last political fiasco, the changing face of Spain, of Europe. He was knowledgeable, he was in industry. Three times a year he had to visit a factory or something in Malaga, he lived in Valencia, which he did not much like, preferred to come back this way, via Alicante and Murcia. He asked her if she was hungry and invited her to lunch. He knew of a little restaurant by the sea near Almeria.

They had an enjoyable meal. He was generous, enjoyed himself, enjoyed most talking in English. He tended to be right wing in his thinking, which was no surprise, and over a strong black coffee, which he said he was taking to help him drive, he paid her a compliment. He said he hoped that he would be able to bring up his daughters the way she had been brought up.

She insisted on seeing the photographs of his family which he had tucked in one fold of his wallet. Madre, Padre, Tio, Tia, Sobrinos, Sobrinas, the lot. His wife was plump, once a

pretty face, but definitely plump after four
children: two boys, two girls. The house was a
white villa, with palm trees, a small swimming pool, an electric lawn mower in the
background, everything perfect. He had studied in Madrid, he was happy because he had
achieved what his parents had wanted him to
achieve and what his in-laws had wanted him
to achieve. He was the perfect example of the
perfect young man who had done well. In time
he would be a company director, he would play
golf, he would sail, he would go for trips to
China and South America.

They journeyed on. The mood was mellow,
he switched on his cassette player, Mozart,
Chopin, then he dared put on a disco tape
which he played, she felt, for her sake.

They came to some road repairs where the
surface was just pure dust and he suggested she
wind up her window. For a moment the whole
car was enveloped in a white cloud and it was
terribly hot, and as they sped on down the new
tarmac, he opened the window, she opened
hers and the gust of fresh air came blasting in,
whipping her hair back. Instinctively she lowered the sun visor to look at herself in the van-
ity mirror, and, for a second, a split second,
caught sight again of the woman in the back.
There was no mistaking the face with the
black hair. But it had no eyes.

Jacinta's ghost, sitting right there behind her in the back seat? Her new friend was busy driving and did not notice her discomfort. She crossed her legs, her tanned thigh looking silky and pure and vulnerable right there in the intimacy of his clean car, and she saw him glance, she watched his fingers nervously tap out the rhythm of the music. She could take this man to bed with her if she wanted, she would enjoy giving him a little thrill, a little change from his plump wife whom he must have got used to after four children.

"Will you reach Valencia tonight?" she asked.

"Oh, no. I usually stop in a hotel somewhere on the way. Murcia, some place like that."

"Murcia?" she repeated, as though that place was of particular interest to her.

"There is a lovely hotel there built within a palm grove with individual chalets around a swimming pool."

"Sounds terrific." She played it correctly, the envy.

"You could stay there as well, as my guest," he said, very tentatively, his very manner, his very voice hoping she would refuse yet desiring that she would accept.

"What about your wife?" she asked.

Slam in there, girl, the direct question, either he was involving himself or he was not.

She was the mature girl, the one who could handle a situation without him having to worry, the prostitute of experience. A free meal and board and her body in exchange. It's what he wanted, what was acceptable. He was a Latin, it happened. It had happened before, he couldn't be that naive.

"It is not always necessary for me to tell her everything I do, all my adventures. A man has to have a life of his own, his own secrets, just as much as a woman does."

The bargain was sealed. There was no point in discussing it further, all she had to do was be nice, come up to expectations and, looking at him sideways, at the way his black hair curled behind his ears, at his carefully shaven sideboards, the line of his neck, his particularly dark-skinned sensitive hands, she decided that he would probably be quite fun, or at least she would make sure he was. Besides, she had never had herself a middle-aged, middle-class Spaniard.

And now that she felt secure that she had a friend next to her, felt safe, she dared turn round, as casually as she could, to stare at the manifestation in the back.

But of course it had gone. Her imagination, her subconscious playing tricks. She was running away from an image of Jacinta, and the image wasn't going to be discarded that quickly. That was all.

The hotel was right in the middle of a quaint, dusty, nearly ugly town, of high ochre walls and winding streets. They turned into a crowded car park through wrought iron gates and were met by a uniformed attendant who took care of the car.

As she stepped out she felt a little awkward in her cut-off jeans, she had dressed for a lorry driver and had ended up with an executive.

He did not seem to mind, if he did he was certainly polite enough not to make her feel it. She did have a dress, one dress, the blue non-crease fabric, and with her gold necklace and the gold earrings Chantal had given her, a little make up and her leather sandals, she'd manage to look presentable.

They signed in. His name was Luis Ayola Molina. Hers was not.

The receptionist asked for the passports, Luis told him it would not be necessary, the man understood. No winks, discretion itself, it was the only hotel in Spain she had been in where there was silence, where people did not shout, did not scream, where innuendo was general practice.

They followed the bell-boy out into the gardens and, under very tall palm trees by an oval shaped swimming pool all lit up, bright blue, they were shown to Chalet 15.

The bell-boy put her old suitcase down on top of her host's brand new pigskin, and closed the door after accepting an obviously generous tip.

"You have a bath and change while I make a call," he said.

"OK," she replied, and she stood on tiptoe to give him a brief loving kiss on the lips.

"Thank you for everything so far," she said, and grabbing her suitcase went into the black tiled bathroom where she discreetly closed the door.

She turned on the water and pressed her ear to the door and heard the tinkle of the telephone bell. He would be ringing his wife. A puncture, a delay, an excuse, so many excuses could be made on such a long journey. A faulty car part, an unexpected business proposal which had to be followed through.

Would she care, his wife, with four children and a nanny and a mother-in-law? Would she care? She might have a lover and be grateful.

Zuke hung her dress up on the shower curtain rail and looked at herself in the mirror. She was in a pretty filthy state. She turned off the tap, curious to listen. He was asking after the children, after his mother, saying something about a deal. He'd be home tomorrow evening, all being well. And after he hung up he whistled, the disco tune, their tune. Perhaps he was falling in love with her, which would be nice.

She had a shower and when she was out and had dried herself and combed her hair, she looked like the attractive girl she had known before. She wrapped herself in the oversize bath towel, sarong style, and opened the door.

He was sitting on the bed, by the telephone, with his back to her.

"The bathroom is free," she said.

He made it, via his suitcase to pick up his leather travelling case, electric razor and after shave, without looking at her.

The doubt had set in. Maybe talking to his wife, maybe hearing the children's little voices in the background had done it, maybe it would be a night with a bolster between them and a prayer asking the Virgin Mary for forgiveness. Guilt was in the shiftiness of his eyes.

She threw herself on the bed, unwrapped the white towel and lay there exposed, while he showered on the other side of the closed door. He could come in now and have her, she was all his for the asking, but he wouldn't, not till after dinner, not till after lights out.

She smiled. She had considered rape, now she was considering rejection, again. Well she would do the decent thing and not frighten him. She would seduce him slowly, quietly, gently. It would be a challenge. She really quite liked him. He had nice long legs, long feet, and sensuous lips, and somewhere in there was hidden a lustful body.

She slipped on her blue dress quickly, combed her hair through again and again and wiped over her sandals with the corner of the curtain. She lifted the top of his suitcase and looked through his belongings. Two shirts, a grey suit, ties, socks, a pair of black shoes, two books, one a translation of Raymond Chandler, the other a missal, which was a surprise, his wife no doubt packing a few saints in to protect him from such as herself, and an all-purpose mother of pearl handled penknife.

For no reason at all an image of Jacinta, smiling, came to mind. Was her ghost egging her on to be evil? Had she been taken over by the girl's spirit in order to corrupt sweet gentle middle-class executives?

As she heard the shower being turned off, she moved away from the suitcase and stood in front of the mirror, combing her wet hair through again. It was getting dryer. He was shaving now, the buzz of the electric razor making a surprising din in the bathroom.

Near the telephone he had left his address book. Not as new as the other things, but new enough, black leather with his initials on it.

She flicked it open, guiltily, addresses and telephone numbers in a meticulous handwriting. He was an accountant, had to be, in publishing it seemed, educational books. Well, she could cope with that, surprise him. Maybe they'd spend the evening discussing the works of Cervantes and Becquer. She'd get him round to De Sade eventually.

It was the comfort of that double bed and the smell of the cologne she was pouring on herself which was turning her on. She twirled round in front of the mirror, which she had not done for years, and decided that she was quite pretty, feminine anyway. Maybe she should give up the butch jeans, health girl approach. Maybe she should get married to such as he and settle down and have a million children.

The door opened and he came out all dressed. He'd taken his clothes in with him, carefully pressed beige trousers, polished brown casual shoes with gold buckles, a long-sleeved brown shirt, a beige jacket with a brown handkerchief in the top pocket to match the rest.

"Hungry?" he asked.

He put his wallet, bulging with credit cards, in his pocket and at the door paused, held her by the arm, then kissed her gently on the forehead.

He kissed his daughter like that every night, she was sure.

"You look very attractive," he said.

What he was really telling her was that, to his surprise, she had made herself look more presentable than he had expected.

He held her hand all the way down the garden path, and they paused to look at a couple of nut brown men swimming in the spotlit pool. Then they went into the restaurant building, all modern, with a balcony overlooking the pool, half-empty, where musak filled the air just softly enough to make lonely diners feel more comfortable.

The menu came in four languages with a little flag insignia to tell people what language they were reading. She glanced down the English menu and compared it to the Spanish, there were the usual funny mistakes, "Revolted Eggs," "Rape on Grill." They laughed about them.

"What would you like to drink?"

"I'll let you choose," she said, demurely, and watched him go through the wine tasting act as though she'd never done the journey before.

"Tell me about your family," she then asked, for openers.

It was the one thing he really didn't want to talk about, but she knew it was on his mind, so if they got that out of the way quickly they'd be making progress.

His father was a lawyer and his brother was

a lawyer and his sister was a doctor and he was in publishing because his uncle was in publishing, and so it went on. Stability, respectability, education and money all the way, he had been an officer in the army, had not liked it, spent his holidays abroad.

She then asked him if he had many lovers before getting married. It was none of her business, but he was too polite to say so. One or two. An English girl, a Danish girl, he was Mr. Macho like all the others. He was careful not to insult, careful to avoid making the point that foreign girls were for fun, the Spanish girls were all virgins. She might make him regret that, might just dig her nails into his neck leaving telltale scratches for his wife to see when she next scrubbed his back in their all-tiled master bathroom.

"Tell me about yourself," he said.

She did. Three quarters of a bottle of the wine consumed, mostly by him. The orphan story now, deserted by father, admitting the Harvard professor was a lie. Brought up penniless by mother. She had crossed the whole of America, had never found the right man, longed somehow to be taken care of, didn't want marriage. Loved Spain, adored Spain, had this ambition to live somewhere along the coast.

She could see herself being set up in her

apartment in Puerto Lucena. It would be such a convenient stop-over between Valencia and Malaga on his business trips.

There was a lull in the conversation between dishes, embarrassing, so, in desperation she asked a question she did not want answered.

"Have you ever heard of a book entitled *A Discourse on the Reality of the Occult*?"

He had not. "Does the occult hold a fascination for you?"

"No, not at all," and thankfully, steered the conversation round to art and paintings and her visit to the Prado and they drifted into an intellectual intercourse which she felt dangerous for he was on his second brandy which might well be for Dutch courage, and could also put him to sleep.

"Do you have many conversations like this with your wife?" she asked, to jar him.

"No . . . not many. She was an art student, but since the family . . ."

"I've often wondered whether the Latin male considered intellectual intercourse with the opposite sex as sinful as sexual intercourse? To me it sometimes seems more lethal."

"It had never occurred to me," he admitted.

She had made him nervous, brought him down to earth.

A little wild eyed, unsettled, like a man on

OUIJA

whom the death sentence had been irrevocably passed, he looked round for the head waiter to get the bill, looked at his watch and smiled, nervously.

It would be very quick. She had spoilt the joy, there would be no walk around the gardens, or a lunatic swim in the pool, or a warm up in a discoteca. She had hit the wall of respectability head on, the digital watch was saying "time for bed."

The waiter took hours to bring the bill, which he signed. They listened in silence to the musak. She felt sleepy, imagined the bed, imagined him next to her. Would he dare wear pyjamas? She'd laugh at him if he did.

She deliberately took his hand as they left the restaurant, but when he saw the bar full of people, he steered her clear, reminding her that there was a refrigerator in their room full of drink, if she really wanted one.

And then above the tumult, above the voices in the bar, she distinctly heard, as he heard, his name being called out.

"Ola, Luis!"

His hand first tightened round hers, then disengaged itself quickly. He turned round holding his breath, anguish in his eyes. Standing by the hotel entrance was a small fattish man, sixty, grey suit, white shirt, grey tie, a cigar between stubby fingers, looking at them with some amazement.

Next to him was a heavy lady of the same age, black and white spotted dress, crocodile handbag, hair so lacquered that it could be a wig, incredulous.

Luis swallowed. He did not swallow for air, for breath, he swallowed for life. He was rooted, unable to move, unable to utter a word.

"Hombre!" The man said coming towards him, "Introduce us to your friend." Luis was unable to. He was a little boy, a child, caught red handed with his trousers down doing something he shouldn't.

"Ola," Zuke said, stepping forward. *"Me llama Zuleika, soy la prima de Luis, de America . . ."* It was an attempt to save the day, to save him. It could just be that she was a long lost cousin from across the seas.

The man was amused. "Good try, *chica*, but I think we know all Luis's relatives," he said in good English, "This is my wife, we are Luis's parents-in-law, his wife's mother and father, *comprendes*?"

There was no pretence with these people. There was going to be neither hypocrisy, nor release. Luis had been caught.

"We saw you dining together, you are in a chalet opposite our own, across the swimming pool."

The woman was staring at her, examining her from top to toe. She was furious. Indignation was steaming under her make up, she clearly did not even want to be standing in the same room as her.

"We know you are staying here because we checked. My wife checked." The older man was in a way excusing his wife's behaviour. He would not have checked himself, a question of pride, of decorum, of understanding.

The woman was still staring at her. "He is a family man," she said in a strong but understandable accent. "He has four children!"

"So that makes me a criminal?"

"*Chica*, let us not get angry," the older man said.

Luis, at her side, was still rooted, still trying to get his breath.

"Well Luis? Do you want me to go sleep in some other room? Pretend I never existed?" she asked.

"I think it would be better, yes, if we did that. I'll try and get you another room."

"Thanks," she said, and an unexpected anger surged up. She was being treated like dirt, the use of the word *"chica"* was somehow denigrating, she was being insulted in front of people whose pride was supreme.

Well she was proud too. "You can't ditch m

that easily, Luis," she said. "I do have feelings."

"Nothing has happened," Luis said weakly to his in-laws, ignoring her. "Nothing. I just picked her up on the way, between Malaga and Almeria, she was also going to Valencia. She has no money. It was a gesture."

Unbelievably the woman swung her arm, heavy with gold jewellery, up from the hip to slam the back of her hand hard across Luis's face. Here was the Latin temperament let loose in public, the bourgeois family causing a scandal in a respectable hotel foyer!

The hand came up again and struck her across the left cheek.

"Mujer!" the husband shouted, restraining another possible assault, but by then Zuke had kicked hard at the woman's ankle, turned and stormed out into the garden.

She rubbed her cheek and walked down the path fully aware that the whole world was watching her. If it hadn't hurt so much, if she hadn't looked the part of the poor girl picked up for a quick screw, she would have felt a lot better, but right now she was humiliated.

She reached the chalet only to realise she didn't have the key. Uncontrollable rage welled up at the conceit of the woman, at the arrogance of the two men.

She wasn't a whore!

She turned and saw the faces at the restaurant windows. However educated and elegant these people were supposed to be they were as curious as fishwives.

Father-in-law and goody-two-shoes were now coming towards her, the former holding the latter by the arm. The tearful schoolboy being led by the headmaster. How could a man with whom she had chosen to sleep because she held him in sufficient respect suddenly turn to jelly? He was the weakest thing she'd seen on God's earth. The father had the key, he pushed her aside, gently, but all the same pushed her, opened the door and taking her by the elbow ushered her into the chalet.

"Now, you please take your things, your suitcase, your clothes, and I drive you to another hotel."

He dug his hand into his jacket pocket, brought out his wallet and counted out ten thousand pesetas in green notes. "To help you," he said handing it to her. "I hope you can accept this as a gift. You are an intelligent girl."

"Are *you* going to stay with me at this other hotel then?" she asked. The offer of the hush money was incredible.

"Now *chica*, be reasonable. We are a well known family in this area, we have our reputation, you must understand."

73

"I have a reputation too . . ."

She opened the door wide, screamed at the top of her voice "Get out! Both of you! Get out!"

They hesitated, Luis petrified, looking at his in-law for guidance. Other chalet doors opened, the restaurant balcony was crowded, waiters stood with trays poised, mouths open, they had never witnessed a scene like it.

And then it was as though time suddenly stood still: a similar feeling to the one she had had when seeing Jacinta's reflection in the car mirror. A timelessness where the people seemed like dummies, motionless, and in the swimming pool there was a girl, floating, an Ophelia like creature, floating on her back, no garlands, but black hair, a white dress . . . Jacinta again, smiling at her, beckoning.

It lasted less than a second, a fantasy image in her mind. Then she was seized by a quite demoniacal desire to hurt these upstart people.

Father-in-law was holding her firmly by the wrist and closing the door again.

"*Chica!*" he now warned, "I can have you arrested, you know that. My brother-in-law is a lawyer. . . ."

They'd do it, they'd have her put away in some crumby jail, locked up, certified as a lunatic tart to save the family name.

A remarkable calmness now overtook her,

she felt herself changing, someone else's smile dancing on her own lips, her eyes staring at Luis, at the older man, as she had never stared at anyone, as though she had an inner knowledge of the doom that awaited them. It was a metamorphosis of the mind, a metempsychosis, and she slowly, very slowly, disengaged her wrist, took two steps back from the men, slipped off her right shoulder strap, her left, let her dress drop to the floor, she kicked off her sandals, stepped out of her slip and stood there naked, stark naked.

Then she gave a piercing scream, tore the door open, hurled herself out into the garden, plunged headlong into the pool, swam down to the complete blue silence at the bottom, aware only of white bubbles rising above her, and surfaced seconds later for air.

A thousand faces were looking at her, then all the lights went out and she heard splashes, felt powerful arms get hold of her, metal buttons pressed against her skin, a bearded face scratching hers, she couldn't struggle. She was being lifted, carried to the shallow end in the dark, by one of the waiters, or the porter, a loyal servant of the hotel saving the reputation of the establishment. A bath towel was wrapped round her. She was surrounded by men, the management, being led back to the chalet. The lights went on, the door closed.

"What do you want?" the father-in-law was saying. "I am sorry I insulted you. I am sorry. I was not thinking. What do you want. What do you *want*?"

She sat down on the bed, shivering, not from cold but from emotion, someone handed her a brandy.

"I was invited to spend the night with Luis, I think he should honour that invitation," she said, quite calmly.

It was beautiful, the way she handled it. Nude and wet, she was the serene water goddess commanding respect. She was a man's mistress and she was to be treated as such.

"You are right, you are right," the father-in-law said.

"I have been grievously insulted, Señor," she continued, "I am not a *puta*, Luis happens to be my lover, I think you should allow him to behave like a man."

"Of course, of course."

Everyone left, the door closed. She was alone.

She went to the bathroom, looked at herself for a long time in the mirror. She had not changed but had to admit that for a while, for a good little while, she had felt that she had been taken over.

Her behaviour had been quite uncharacteristic, the pride, the fiery anger. That had not been her.

She slid into bed after helping herself to more brandy and stretched out under the sheets in the peace of the dimly lit room.

Where was Luis now? Begging forgiveness? Ringing up his wife to explain his innocence? The door opened quietly and she closed her eyes pretending to be asleep.

It was Luis. Would he collect his belongings and disappear? He started padding about the room, went into the bathroom for his razor, stooped to find his shoes under the bed.

"Luis," she whispered, "Do you have to go?"

"I woke you? I am sorry."

She switched on the brighter light and wished she hadn't. He had been crying, his eyes were puffed and red, his face drawn.

"Turn the light off, please," he asked.

She switched the light off and stretched out her hand for his. To her surprise he crumbled onto the bed next to her, clung onto her and started sobbing.

A tenderness came over her, and again she felt she was acting, not being herself. She felt a peaceful expression steal across her face, her long slender hands stroked his head, his hair, it was a strange sensation which was foreign to her. As she rocked him she felt the warm closeness of his body excite her. She wanted him, she wanted this man, and she kissed him gently on the forehead, then between the eyes, then on the lips.

"*Oh no . . . niña . . .*" he murmured.

"You have already been judged and have already paid for the crime, so why not commit it?"

The phrase was hardly hers, it came from some other mind, some other voice, but because he was Latin, or because he had no will power, or because she had somehow become irresistible, the love making that developed was of an ecstatic nature she had never experienced before.

It was the wine, the violence, the swim, the sadness, the forbidden fruit.

He was gentle and forceful and fullsome and patient and sensuous. It lasted an hour, maybe more. He moved across the bed, he carried her around the room, at a moment when she thought it would be all over he placed her under the cold shower and dampened both their enthusiasms so that it could go on again. He made her feel smaller, more vulnerable, more feminine, more sensuous, and when it was finally over she heard herself sighing, and whimpering, which she had never done before. He laid her gently on the bed and covered her with the sheet. And she closed her eyes and allowed herself to drift into a very deep sleep.

* * *

She was wakened by a gentle tap on the door.

She sat up, looked around the dimly lit room, the only light coming through the slats of the metal blinds.

Quickly she took in the scene, the situation. Luis's suitcase, open, his clothes on the floor, the untidiness of the lovemaking in evidence everywhere.

"Come in," she said.

A waiter with a breakfast for two.

He put the tray down on the table by the bed and left, discreetly, as though he had seen nothing.

The bathroom door was closed. Luis presumably in there shaving, having a bath, getting ready for his terrible day.

She'd help him out. She wouldn't abandon him if he wanted her, she would stand by him, give him support.

She stretched, yawned. She was herself again, Zuleika from Glendale, Arizona.

Then she sniffed something strange in the air, a sickly smell, which somehow frightened her. She got out of bed, tried the bathroom door. It was locked.

"Luis?"

No keyhole, no outside bolt. It was one of those inside locking devices. She knocked hard, really hard, and waited . . . Nothing. She went to his suitcase, the long penknife had gone. She took a series of deep breaths, poured herself out a coffee, black, drank it, and picked up the telephone.

"*Por favor*. The manager, quickly. An emergency."

She would have to remain very calm. Slowly, deliberately slowly, she slipped on her blue dress, and her sandals, and sat down on the edge of the bed.

After a few moments there was a knock at the door, she opened up, the manager himself was there with one of his security men.

She indicated the door with a look which explained enough. They tried it. On either side of the handle were two special screws she had not noticed. The security man got to work immediately.

They opened up, were too preoccupied with what they were doing to think of keeping her from seeing what they all expected to find. But the sight was not what anyone could have foreseen. Luis had made sure that he would never touch another woman again. The self mutilation was an insane ritual self massacre.

From his contorted body lying in a pool of blood on the floor, the scene could easily enough be worked out. He had gagged himself so that his agonised screams would not wake her up. He had tied his penis with a length of cord to the shower rail, hacked at himself and fallen backwards leaving the part dangling, then he had slit open the veins of both arms and allowed himself to bleed to death.

The manager turned round and vomited. The security man turned and just made it to the garden. She remained quite still, unmoved, looking at the carnage. She felt an incredible strength building up within her, a strength brought about by a victory, by rejoicing that justice had been done.

And as she stared at the obscenity dangling above the bath she realised she was smiling. What had she become?

CHAPTER FOUR

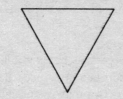

CHANTAL received the two missing sections of the book within an hour of each other.

On the morning of Jacinta's funeral she had been given a package by the girl's grandmother with the explanation that two other similar packages had been found in her room together with the instructions that they should be delivered to the Englishman at his hotel and the American girl at her apartment.

Chantal had unwrapped the last ninety pages of the book and, glancing through it, had decided that it was just another occult volume guessing about the afterlife. Then the middle section was delivered by one of the men from the agency managing Zuke's apartment block, and shortly after a porter from Warren's hotel arrived with the opening chapters, so that she could now piece it all together.

The notes from Zuke and Warren surprised her. They admitted so much fear.

Dear Chantal

The enclosed was given me this morning by one of Jacinta's cousins. I have not read it, but leafed through it enough to feel oppressed, so much so that by the time you receive this I will have left. I do not know where I am going, but I need to get away from here and from the atmosphere created by our playing the ouija.

Frankly I feel haunted by Jacinta and this part-book has made it worse. I will write to you in a few days time from wherever I decide to settle.

Love Zuke.

The other note, more English, less honest, typically Warren, pretended confidence.

My Dear Chantal,

A brief note to thank you for your marvellous hospitality over the past few days. The enclosed was given me by Jacinta's grandfather this morning and I thought I would leave it with you as you believe in the subject more than I do. The whole episode was certainly an experience I would not like to repeat.

My very best wishes always,

Warren.

Chantal sat at the ouija table piecing the book together with Sellotape, cutting the thin gummy paper carefully, and making quite a neat job of it.

She ran her fingers over the spine, the gold lettering of the title, and the author's name.

A Discourse on the Reality of the Occult
Armando Valdez Ortega

Events would follow now, strange unpredictable events would start fitting into a pattern which might make little sense at first but eventually would add up to a unique revelation. She felt this, deep down, without being able to explain it, and the thought was a comforting one. She knew that she was no longer alone.

She put the book in the middle of the table, placed both her hands on top of it and closed her eyes in meditation. One of the passages she had read immediately came to mind.

At all times one should be open to the receiving of esoteric signals and messages which may need less interpretation than expected. Communications from the dead are never complicated.

She picked up the book and held it to her forehead and in her mind's eye just saw that name again, Armando Valdez Ortega.

It was the first proof that the spirit who had contacted them had really existed, and what was more he had written a book about communicating with the dead. It had to be an exceptional set of circumstances.

She went to her bookcase and consulted her Spanish *Encyclopedia*, *Chambers Biographical Dictionary*, the French *Larousse*, but in none was the name Valdez Ortega mentioned, which was disappointing.

Before anything else, therefore, she should find out more about this man, get some inkling as to why Jacinta's gift was an English version, why, if he had been translated from the Spanish, he wasn't better known?

On the first page of the book below the title, was the publisher's name and address. Editorial Grapos. Calle del Coffre 3. Madrid.

She would go. She didn't have to, she could ring up, write a letter, wait for an answer, go to Malaga, even to the library, but it was an excuse to visit the capital which she loved, a good excuse, her absence for a while would help the village forget her connection with the dead Jacinta which, she had to admit, had unsettled her neighbors.

She started packing, excited by the thought of the journey ahead, of the shopping she would be able to do, of staying in a hotel, which she had not done for so long.

However delightful her home was, however luxurious she had made it, the life around her was rural, indeed very peasant, but then the simple undemanding people she had chosen to mix with over the past five years had helped her survive.

She decided to go by train because it would be ideal for reading the book without interruption, or so she told herself. The Talgo Express from Malaga to Madrid was a little like the genteel travel of her childhood days after the war, nostalgic. At least she was no longer relying on Jacques now.

She was no longer turning instinctively to his memory for advice, no longer praying, for that is what it had become, a sort of prayer, a belief that he was listening from somewhere out there in the oblivion of the dead.

Jacques was beginning to mean less to her, which was sad, yet she firmly believed that this was what he wanted. It was what they all wanted, the dead. "Forget us, forget we ex-

isted, live on without us, live on happily, it is
only a phase anyway."

She believed that. Life being a phase. It was
not a transition, not a bridge from one life to
another, but a phase, an evolutionary phase,
and she believed in reincarnation and other
lives to follow. Which was why the ouija fascinated her so.

Jacques was somewhere else now, whether
they would ever meet again was of course pure
speculation. She had more than enjoyed his
love, his devoted love, she had known what
many other couples had never known, a perfect understanding between husband and wife.

Maybe, somewhere in his subconscious, he
had known his life would be short and he had
been more intense about everything.

Did we all know, in our subconscience, how
long we would live?

She should ask the ouija that. Was she beginning to believe in the image she had created
of herself? The medium, the clairvoyant? And
what would Jacques think of her fantasies?

Jacques did not matter any more. She had
been spoilt by him of course, educated by him
and spoilt. For twenty-five years he had been a
hard-working accountant in a Paris fashion
house and it had corrupted them both. She had
been a model, he had married her. "Monsieur
Christian has bought another Leonor Fini,"

"Monsieur Christian is now collecting La-
lique," "Monsieur Christian has decided that
yellow and grey are next year's colours for in-
teriors," and their interior changed yet again.
She'd had no complaints, she'd loved it. He had
given her the life she had sought, had hoped
for, had aimed for. Of course she had dreamed
of marrying a really rich man, a millionaire.
She had read all the novels under the sun while
waiting to walk onto the rostrum, but she had
learned quickly enough that the model girls
who landed the big fish were usually big fish
themselves, one way or another, related, or
connected with money. Occasionally there was
the little urchin girl like herself who really
knew how to use her sex appeal and had the
intelligence to manoeuvre into society, but she
had not had the energy. Manouche had had
the energy and had ended up with the Texan
oil magnate and the yacht, but where had that
got her except to the bottle?

Considering her inborn laziness and lack of
true ambition she had not done badly. She
had remained in fashion longer than most, had
stepped from mannequin to vendeuse, had
earned well, lived in central Paris, had been
the friend of the rich. Her opinion had mat-
tered, as much as Jacques'. The small apartment had become like an antique shop, and he

had always said "If things ever get rough, we can always sell."

And things had got rough: the illness, the too long illness, and the cost of the clinic, then the death, and the year of wandering. She had let herself go deliberately.

It was Louise, another vendeuse, who had never married and was mad anyway, who had insisted she go to a seance to meet Jacques again, to contact Jacques, and she had gone to please her.

It had been such a farce and Louise had been so completely taken in, the tape recorder and speaker under the table, the lighting effects and heavy breathing, it had been unbelievably bad, and Louise had fallen for it all.

Of course the medium knew all about Jacques, Louise had told her everything beforehand without realising it. But it had started a train of thought. If the so called medium could get away with it, so could she herself.

She had not considered the idea seriously until she had held a private auction in the apartment for friends and acquaintances, and one of them had been interested in a little brass box that looked very old because of its faded velvet lining.

She had told the woman that it had once belonged to Napoleon's manservant because when she held it in her hand she got visions of battlefields, and the woman had been very impressed and had said that she must have psychometric powers.

"Of course I have. I can tell you the history of all my objects," she'd boasted, and the woman had immediately handed her an earring. "Can you tell me about this then?" She had made up some fanciful story of it belonging to the Empress Eugenie because it reminded her of one worn in a portrait by Winterhalter. The woman had been astonished.

"I lost the other, could you tell me where it is?"

"You lost it when?" she had asked.

"Many years ago, we were staying with friends in Touraine, in a chateau, it was such beautiful countryside."

She had closed her eyes, demanded silence from everyone, then had pronounced that the woman had lost it while on a picnic.

"I was on a picnic!"

"You lost it in a long meadow, with tall grasses, I can see the place quite clearly, but it is built over now, large farm buildings."

"Does that mean I will never find it?"

"Not unless you dig under the concrete."

The woman had believed her, had gone away happy and had paid a ridiculously high price for the little brass box, and everyone had said she had an obvious future as a clairvoyant with such a rare gift.

Two years later, when furnishing her converted mill, she had bought second hand books by the yard in a shop in Marbella, to fill the bookshelves, all languages, English, French, German, Danish. Among them had been several on the occult. One sleepless night she had thumbed through them and learned about cryptomania, odic energy, psychokinesis—that people wanted to believe in all that mumbo jumbo, wanted to project their souls into another dimension.

Warren had confirmed this, with the success of his games.

She had begun to dress a little more eccentrically, and had deliberately gathered all the information she could on an old English lady who had been recently widowed. She had noted all the information about her husband, how he had died, his circumstances, the way they had lived in England, and one night she had finally been invited to a dinner party where the old bird was a guest and had launched forth with her psychic divinations.

She had held the woman's hands and told her about her aura and the aura that was always next to her. It had connections with banking, with dogs, bull-terriers, and the woman had started crying and demanded a seance. Instead of a crystal ball or going into a trance she had chosen the ouija to contact the other world. A glass was easy to move, the neo-classic mahogany tripod table with its highly polished surface was ideal. She had cut gothic letters from an old book on manuscripts and then stuck them down and varnished them.

She had told the old widow so many truths that she had insisted on paying her, not in cash but with the gift of a diamond and sapphire brooch, no less. She had had it valued and it was still in her jewellery box ready to be sold the moment it was necessary.

Two other clients had come, fee paying, special appointments. It had not been so easy, but she had got the knack very quickly of finding out what they wanted to hear. People told you what they wanted to hear, it was a question of attentive listening and observation.

The ouija glass, she had to admit, had some-times seemed to move of its own accord, and when Jacinta had joined her the first time it had positively raced around. If you accepted that body electricity could cause objects to move, it was all quite explainable.

What was not explainable was Jacinta's connection with Valdez Ortega, and how she had come by the English translation of the book.

Once settled in the train, a comfortable window seat facing the engine, she opened the book and turned over each page, glancing down it for anything that might catch her eye. She would not be able to read it all and felt that there might be something specific in its contents relevant to Jacinta's suicide.

Some of the passages were totally ridiculous and could be set aside as nonsense invented by an over-imaginative mind, but others were fascinating.

In the middle she found a paragraph boxed in by wavy lines, it concerned metempsychosis, then mentioned the name Jacinta, apparently a fictitious character in another book. She read further and under the next chapter heading, Metempsychosis or the Migration of Souls at Death, she read:

A violent end to life by assassination, suicide or accident is more likely to provide the soul with the necessary impulse to enter a living body than a peaceful, natural death. When we die we go into limbo where one's soul, one's mind can think eternally without interruption. From limbo we can move into an unknown world beyond, which is a progress. We can be reincarnated to live on this earth oblivious of the fact that we have lived before. Or as Metempsychics, reincarnated to live on this earth *fully* aware of what we

were before *and* possessing psychic powers—Sakya Muni, Jesus Christ, as examples.

This was followed by a warning that metempsychosis could only occur under very rare
conditions, those being that the person entered, the live body, be carefully chosen, preconditioned and sufficiently acquainted with
unexpected and unexplainable violent death
not to react adversely to psychic phenomena.

What Chantal found intriguing was that the
author wrote, it seemed, from experience, and
gave the impression that he had experimented
ceaselessly to produce this authoritive text
book on possible communication with the
dead.

Should she now believe that Jacinta's death
was somehow connected with his theories,
that the fictitious Jacinta mentioned was the-
oretical experimentation and that the late, real
Jacinta, had been the practice?

It sent a shiver down her back which she
found exciting. If, for some unknown reason,
Señor Valdez Ortega had chosen *her* as part of
a psychic experiment, she was not sure she
would mind. She would, in fact, find it flattering.

On arriving in Madrid she went straight to a
small hotel in the centre where she had stayed
before, and once refreshed rang up an old friend

who invited her to dinner. She was on a brief shopping spree, nothing more, she explained.

The next day she hailed a taxi and asked for Editorial Grapos, Calle del Coffre 3. The driver had never heard of it, had never heard of the street, had no idea what district it would be in, and his map did not list it.

So she suggested the Biblioteca Nacional and started off on an unexpectedly active day.

She had never met up with historians or scholars before and suddenly she found herself plunged in detailed researches, and discovered in the various academics who were not particularly interested in the occult, a feverish curiosity and an intense determination to save Valdez Ortega, this unknown author, from oblivion.

Countless reference books, bibliographies and publishers' catalogues were consulted, antiquarian bookshops were rung, leads were followed till a collector of the esoteric was eventually traced and an appointment for her to see him made for the next day.

He was not at all what she expected.

Though learned, cultured and wearing glasses, he was neither old, seedy nor buried knee-deep in a dusty study surrounded by ancient tomes. He was young, with good tanned looks, dressed in jeans, and an open neck shirt and bare footed.

The moment of mutual admiration at the front door was cut short by his astonished excitement on seeing the book she handed him.

"This is incredibly rare," he explained. "Only fifty were hand-printed secretly in London after the original Spanish edition was destroyed by the authorities, and of these fifty only a few survived a fire in the author's house. Come through, I'll show you all the documentation I have on him."

At the back of the modern apartment, furnished only with the best of essentials, he had a special air conditioned room for his collection. Shelves were stacked with old manuscripts and archives, on the walls hung astrological charts, a glass case contained psychic research devices including a small Victorian ouija board which fascinated her.

He danced his fingers through the files of a cabinet and pulled out a large envelope of papers and photostats, finding the one he was looking for.

"This is the only biographical material on the man. Remarkably little is known about him because the church did such a good job of obliteration."

He handed her a sheet of typed foolscap headed Ortega.

She read it carefully, though aware that as she did so, he was watching her, considering her approvingly, she sensed, which was flattering, if a little surprising.

Armando Valdez Ortega was born in 1824 in Southern Spain. At nineteen he went to Madrid to study theology. Aged twenty-eight he wrote his first book, a novel which was received by critics and reviewers as outstanding in its originality, a breakthrough into occult romanticism, but was immediately banned by the church and subsequently the Minister of Justice as a flagrant attack on Christian ethics. Translated into several languages and sold under cover with other banned books, political pamphlets and pornography, it enhanced his reputation sufficiently for him to travel to England, where he settled for a while. In 1864, aged forty, he married a rich publisher's widow who professed psychic powers and who encouraged him in his further studies of the occult. In 1872 he wrote *Ensayos Sobre La Realidad Del Ocultismo*, causing a furore. The critic, Leopoldo Aras, in the *Revista de Madrid* wrote: "Valdez Ortega has hurled himself in the abyss of hell; he has published the devil's own doctrine, an incendiary thesis, a profane thesis of such sacrilegious nature that I say 'Let him be excommunicated!' for it is fit and right that he should be so!"

All copies were destroyed by the authorities, though he published an English translation immediately, from his London home. This, however, was also destroyed in a fire a year later.

Following the mysterious death of his wife shortly after, he invested his inheritance in a lengthy and abortive legal action attempting to justify the theories set out in his book. This brought journalistic investigation into his private life and the unproven rumour that he had killed his wife while practising black magic.

Reduced to penury, Valdez Ortega spent the next ten years in dire circumstances, eventually finding some stability teaching Spanish to foreign students. In 1899 a young girl of seventeen was found decapitated in his lodging rooms. He was accused of sorcery and satanic practices, was sentenced to death for her murder and was executed on the 4th July, 1902.

Chantal handed the document back, but her host said she could keep it. He had other copies.

"I don't know your name," he added, ushering her out of the room. "I know you as Madame Daubigny, but that is a little formal."

It was forward of him, but somehow forgivable.

"My friends call me Chantal," she said, "What should I call you?"

"Carlos."

He offered her a coffee, then a little later suggested she should stay for a snack lunch.

The intimacy started when they were drinking wine on the balcony and she stretched out for an olive from a dish she could not reach.

He picked one for her and placed it directly in her mouth.

He asked her many questions, obviously trying to find out her age, and eventually she told him, "I'm forty-three, if that's what's bothering you."

He smiled.

"How old are you?" she asked.

"Thirty-two."

"It shouldn't be a drawback."

They prepared the food together, feeding each other titbits; tomato, anchovy, lettuce, till inevitably they kissed, after which he lost no time, but unzipped the back of her dress, cupped his hands on her breasts and feverishly kissed her.

Taken aback by his impatience, but all the same stimulated, she moved her hand downwards to discover that he had nothing at all under his jeans but a fervent excitement for her.

Manfully, but gently, he picked her up and took her to his bedroom.

Like the rest of the apartment it was furnished with only the bare essentials, in this case a very large mattress on the polished pine floor with an abundance of cushions.

There were no curtains on the windows which were wide open, and she hoped that they were not overlooked.

He was more forceful than was necessary, as though he feared she might suddenly change her mind, and after pulling off his shirt and kicking off his jeans, he stood stark naked and rising, watching as she undressed, taking her time.

It was rather rough love making, more animal than she had ever previously experienced. She closed her eyes, allowed him to take her arms from around his neck and place them firmly above her head, stretching her legs out and moving in on her as though she were some ritual sacrifice. Since he clearly liked his women to be passive, she obliged but at one moment it was too much and she arched her back, bit her lower lip with the oncoming ecstasy, then quite suddenly gasped as he violently thrust forward, jarring her painfully before collapsing on top of her with all his weight.

She had not felt his orgasm, had certainly not reached her own, and was surprised by this strange behaviour.

Hot, she tried to ease him off, but found him unmovably heavy.

"Carlos?" she whispered.

He was pretending that he could not move, so sapped was his energy.

"Carlos, you're hurting," she implored.

No reaction.

Then she felt him inside her, harder than before, swelling it seemed, growing without movement, and it frightened her.

"Carlos?"

As her head was up against the wall and his penis forced right up inside her, she realised she was pinned under him.

She began to panic. She struggled, tried to move her legs, tried to lift him, but every effort was painful and at one moment quite agonising.

Had he lost consciousness?

Was he an epileptic? Had the strange orgasm been some kind of fit?

The panic grew. She knew nothing about this individual, he might be a sick man suffering from God knows what.

She made an effort to relax, breathe slowly,

very slowly, then using all her strength she managed to move to one side so that her head was no longer trapped.

She now pulled herself up and disengaged herself from his stave-like member, slid off the mattress onto the floor and lay there, regaining her breath, staring at the man who had just made love to her, but whose handsome naked body had now turned to a sickly yellow colour.

He was facing the other way so she knelt closer to him, reached out with both hands and lifted his head.

His eyes stared hideously at her and from between tight lips oozed a foamy white liquid. And he had gone quite cold.

She got up immediately, turned him over, searched for his heart, his pulse, felt nothing, put her ear against his chest, listened, but in vain.

He was dead. Her lover, her brief, learned unexpected lover, was dead. Behind the door she found a silk dressing grown which she quickly put on. Then she went to the telephone in the sitting room and dialled the emergency service.

They took their time answering, of course, and when they finally did she found herself helplessly trembling and incapable of being calm. She blurted out her name, his name, his address, repeated several times that he was dead and they asked whether she had contacted his doctor.

"Please send someone round . . ." she begged, and hung up.

Next to the telephone was Valdez Ortega's book. "The person carefully chosen should be preconditioned and sufficiently acquainted with unexpected and unexplainable violent death not to react adversely to psychic phenomena."

CHAPTER FIVE

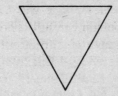

WARREN could not eat the food on the plane, nor could he take an interest in what was happening around him. The expected reaction was beginning to set in, the depression, the breakdown.

Pippa's funeral had been horrendous, the enquiry worse. Nobody he knew had been present, a police officer had even had to read out George's statement because he was in hospital.

He had been so bewildered by the whole business that he was unable to cope with everyone's sympathy and condolences. Eventually, though reluctantly, he had admitted that the only two people he wanted to see, the only friends he had who would understand his innermost fears, were Zuke and Chantal, so he had decided to go away, go back down to Puerto Lucena.

He looked out of the window at the expanse of cotton wool clouds, the bright light blue sky, the dazzling sun. It was a stock picture of heaven, where Pippa might now be.

Or was she in limbo with Valdez Ortega? With Jacinta? The ouija premonition was still unexplainable. *Accident. Saint Stephens.* The ouija had certainly played its part in all these harrowing events.

"We would like you to identify the deceased sir, a matter of routine . . ."

He had been shown Pippa's disfigured remains. He had hardly looked. He recognized the bath robe, the colour of her singed hair. It had been enough.

After that he had visited George in one of the private wards, sheathed in plaster, his neck locked in a pink plastic collar, his head shaved, bruises and cuts on the face exposed.

"I tried to stop her, Warren. I tried to stop her."

The eyes had been fearful, tragic. There had been no need to accuse, to perpetuate the catastrophe.

"Why did she do it?" he'd asked.

"What you said," George tried to explain.

"She loved you, you see. The child was important and she realised that what you said would be true. You would never be sure. She was always very quick, very perceptive and sensitive to situations. I'm sorry."

"How long had it been going on?" he'd asked, "Between you?"

"It hadn't, I promise you. One night stand, old man, on a whim. Had to stay in London, she was lonely, I was lonely . . ."

"On a Saturday night you had to stay alone in London?"

"OK, I didn't. It was pre-arranged . . . it was planned. But will you believe that it didn't come from me? She changed quite suddenly, Warren, surprised me, I can tell you."

"How did she change?"

"Well, I always thought of Pippa as a 'butter wouldn't melt in her mouth' type. Then on Wednesday she invited me out for a drink after the office closed. She invited me, and was quite pushy. I may not have been the only one," George had gone on, "I'm not telling you that to excuse myself. It's just that she became sort of manic, nymphomaniac, threw herself at any man. I shouldn't have taken advantage, but I did. Well you know me, old man, not the type to be able to resist anyone's advances."

"Did she talk about herself at all, her feelings for me?"

"No. She was just ... well ... lustful. Couldn't get to bed quickly enough."

"Was it as though someone else had taken over her mind?"

George had looked at him curiously. "Funny you should say that. That idea did occur to me, but not when we were together, only the morning of her death, only when you'd come in. Her reaction was quite demented, quite frightening. I was frightened."

He'd left the ward after that, taken the lift down, had walked out into the warm summer street and found his way home, which had been terrible without her.

He'd realised he wouldn't be able to think straight in London. George in hospital, George's wife deploring the affair as though it could be put right, his parents seeing the suicide as lunacy, insanity.

He had gone to the office and an hour of it had been enough, the embarrassment caused by his presence.

No one had been capable of handling the situation. He'd gone to a pub alone, somewhere he'd seen a man who reminded him of George and had wondered what Pippa had seen in him, what had George got that he hadn't? Oh grief, he hadn't wanted to stay in London where the sickness would remain with him, the nausea of the mind. Pippa's mother's repetitive question "Why? Why should she do it?" had got on his nerves so much that he had blurted out, "She was having an affair with my boss, *that's* why! She was having an affair with any male she could lay her hands on!"

He hadn't meant it to hurt, but she had gone on at him for too long, blaming him, blaming him because there was no one else to blame, and he was blaming Pippa, hating her for being as unfaithful to him as he had been to her, because he could not face the fact that something had got into her which could not be explained.

He'd booked his flight, sent Chantal a telegram, and now was here.

The plane started its descent, the sight of the clear blue Mediterranean and the white and ochre buildings of Malaga brought instant relief. He now had a longing to be back with Zuke and Chantal, and whatever crazy ideas they might have about the supernatural were better than what he had recently been through.

Once past customs he waited for his bags, one he'd packed hurriedly with an assortment of clothes, the other his holiday suitcase he had not even opened.

There was no one to meet him, so he hired a taxi and settled back to enjoy the familiar scenery and the welcome heat.

At Chantal's villa he found the gate locked.

No one answered the bell, and the anxiety started again.

On the same day Chantal boarded the Talgo express for Malaga, drained of energy, drained of everything.

After relentless interrogations, pointedly embarrassing encounters with Carlos's relatives, endless sleepless nights in a claustrophobic hotel, the police had allowed her to return home, and now she settled down in a corner seat and closed her eyes, hoping for at least a few hours' peace.

But the journey turned out to be a hideous nightmare. As soon as the train started moving she felt herself slip into a state of semi-consciousness in which unknown landscapes and characters invaded her mind.

The scenery that shot by the window changed colours and seasons. As they travelled across La Mancha, which was as timeless as always, she saw things she had never seen before which she knew could not exist, oppressive shadows, phantom figures rising from the earth, white shapes floating in the fields which were somehow terrifying.

As they neared the Sierra Moreno, it got worse. Each tunnel seemed to be the entrance to a new hell and the people around her stopped moving, but were still, deadly, like wax works figures. When she tried to move herself, she realised she was paralysed. She wanted to scream for help but no sound came out of her mouth. By making a great effort she managed a movement.

How could you keep moving physically on a train, other than walking up and down the corridors?

She tried this. She walked the train's length, disturbing people, stepping over suitcases, but even then, as she reached the end of one carriage and found the access door locked she was blinded by vibrant splashes of light and, feeling sick, felt herself sink into a bottomless depression. She thought she was dying, yet knew she was not.

Aware that it might be some form of psychic manifestation, she stopped fighting it, accepting the hallucinations as a new experience which would be beneficial.

She went back to her seat, which was home, with its comfort and relative safety. She closed her eyes and slipped into another trance, the train rattling strangely, like an ancient coach, and on opening her eyes she saw that they were passing through a station crowded with people in costumes, crinolines, bonnets, parasols, mantillas, the men with caped coats and top hats.

She was travelling through the past. Was she

someone else then? Could she be someone else?

Names of importance came to mind, the writers Pardo Bazan, Pereda, Perez Galdos, Generals Pavia and Serrano. President Castelar, The King, Fernando the Seventh. She recalled faces, the lawyers Sanchez and Armenta, Leopoldo Aras who had denounced her, Blancovaras who had judged her.

Her? Denounced her? She was recalling someone else's memory. But whose?

She looked down. All this time she had been holding, clutching, Valdez Ortega's book.

Could it be psychometry? Had Valdez ever made this journey from Madrid to Malaga, was this what she was reliving?

She concentrated now, no longer frightened, she looked out of the window, scanned the scenery for details, but there were electric wires and modern roads, another station, normal, everything normal. She held the book more tightly, wanted to go through the experience again.

She opened it at random, the page where she had stuck the two sections together, a passage she had already read.

A violent end to life by assassination, murder, suicide or accident is more likely to provide the soul with the necessary impulse to enter a living body than a peaceful, natural death. Thus executed criminals have a greater chance to make the extraordinary journey, as in the past did many so-called witches burnt at the stake.

Valdez Ortega had been executed. Jacinta had committed suicide. She lowered the book to rest her eyes and felt the oppression return. This time she did not resist it, but closed her eyes and let her mind travel.

It was an inward journey, like entering her own brain through a cavity behind the forehead. Moving swiftly, silently down a dark passage she emerged in an ill lit white room in the centre of which was a fearful machine.

It was a vicious, torturous device invented to inflict slow and painful strangulation to the victim. It was the garotte.

A blindfold was tied round her eyes from behind as brutish hands pulled her back against the post. The pain she felt was round her wrists as thick ropes bound her tightly so that she would not escape.

Then she heard the metallic click of death, the thick iron ring around her throat tightening, already causing her to gasp for breath.

They left her standing for what seemed hours, she heard a pointless religious incantation, could imagine the priest in moth eaten soutane with dog-eared prayer book standing before her, eyes raised up to heaven on her behalf.

Then there was silence, a shuffling movement behind her, a snapping noise, an incredible pain as she felt her bones splintering, the crushing of the spine, blood flooding up into her eyes.

Violent, hideous death, all in the space of her skull. Then nothing.

She came out of it, stunned and exhausted, a railway official gently tapping her on the shoulder.

"El terminus, Malaga, *Señora."*

She had slept all the way then, dreamt of the garotte, a nightmare due to everything she had read on Valdez Ortega. It was nothing more.

She stood up, collected her belongings and left the pleasant station with its bank of flowers on the platforms, and hailed a taxi.

Sitting in the back, comfortably, she ran her fingers over her neck and felt the weal where the iron ring had tightened and strangled her. From her handbag she took out her small round mirror. There it was, an ugly red and white scar clearly showing where the sharp edge of the ring had cut into the skin. It hurt when she touched it and in no way could have been inflicted by anything she was wearing.

So she had suffered through Valdez Ortega's execution, and carried the marks to prove it. She sat back and stared at the calm sea to her left. "The person carefully chosen should be preconditioned . . ." She had been chosen. For reasons she could not know, she was now sure that she had been chosen by the ouija spirit of Valdez Ortega to be prepared for something exceptional.

She wanted to tell someone, urgently wanted to tell someone who would understand and not think her mad. But Jacinta was dead, Warren had gone and unlikely to return, Zuke, her only real friend gone too, for an indefinite period.

Zuke got through the ordeal of the inquest on Luis's death in unexpected comfort.

In order to keep adverse publicity down to the minimum, the hotel wisely put a chalet at her disposal for however long it took for the police to complete their enquiries. So for four days she was wined and dined free, slept in luxury and was even able to sunbathe by the swimming pool, admiring waiters recharging her glass of wine whenever she smiled at them.

A plainclothes detective spent a whole morning and part of an afternoon taking down her statement, then cross-questioning her, but once he had satisfied himself that she was as innocent as she claimed, he simply asked her to stay in the district and make herself available in case his report did not satisfy his superiors.

She never saw Luis's in-laws again, was not interviewed by reporters, she did not request a lawyer as there seemed to be no need and one morning the hotel manager told her that the police had phoned through and that she was free to leave.

A hotel car drove her to Almeria and from there she took a bus for Puerto Lucena.

She did not go to her apartment to see whether her belongings had been collected and the place let to someone else, but started straight up the mountain road to Chantal's.

Happy to be out in the open, she started the walk at a brisk pace, enjoying the freedom of the open spaces, but was soon offered a lift by the local baker. It was from him that she learnt that Chantal had not been seen for several days, that it was believed she had gone away, and this triggered off an unexpected anxiety.

The baker dropped her off at the entrance of the village and she walked on through up the narrow streets, past the church and down the steep cobbled hill.

From some distance away she saw Chantal's

gate and she thought she recognised Warren's familiar figure leaning against the wall.

As she got closer and saw his two suitcases she felt so elated that she started running, then stopped on hearing the sound of an engine behind her and turned to see Chantal waving at her from the back of a taxi.

All three of them, it appeared, had arrived from different points of departure at the very same time, an extraordinary coincidence, unless they wanted to believe that fate had taken a hand in their destinies.

It was a question of piecing it together, the jig-saw of occurrences which could not be ignored or written off as just chance.

Warren was loath to admit it but the starting point had been his challenge to the ouija, followed by each of them becoming involved in unpleasant deaths.

Chantal insisted that all three of them were subject to the passage in Valdez's book referring to persons being preconditioned to the supernaturally unexpected. To accept that explanation meant to believe in everything Warren had scoffed at from the day he had invented the Tarot game and launched Swifts onto a money spinning range of products based on the credulity of the simple minded.

Now Chantal was insisting that they consult the ouija again, put their heads in the lion's mouth to see what would happen, what advice they would receive. He did not want to do that.

"Why?" Chantal was asking. "Is it that you are afraid of what may happen or that you are afraid of facing a totally new life concept?"

He thought about it, was careful not to answer without analysing his deepest feelings.

They were sitting on the patio watching the evening sun go down. Zuke had prepared a snack meal but no one was eating, none of them was hungry.

"I suppose I'm afraid of going mad, because to believe that we can be in direct contact with the dead, that our actions can be motivated by the dead, is madness!"

"I think you're afraid of not being your own boss any more," Zuke said, perceptively, "You're an ambitious young man and if the world we knew and understand turned out to be a fragment of a much vaster system, then the ladder which you have climbed suddenly has quite a few more rungs."

"We could not be on the same ladder as others, though," Chantal pointed out. "If we have been chosen it is because it has been decided that we can contribute something which others cannot, it is because we are, in some way or other, different."

He was a guest in her house, the argument would go on for ever, the most sensible thing was to show willing and sit at the ouija table to please her.

If nothing happened then he could relax, forget, start life anew. If she was right then the sooner he learnt the laws of the supernatural, the better. It was like being back at school and threatened with a beating. Best to get it over, get it over quickly.

They waited till it was dark, then moved to the dining room. Chantal lit several candles, placed a crystal tumbler in the centre of the marble table and they sat around it placing the tips of their fingers on the base of the glass.

For quite a while nothing happened, then it started to shake. They looked at each other, Chantal closed her eyes to concentrate, then said, "We are in contact, we feel you. Have you a name?"

The glass started a long journey to and fro across the table and Warren felt a sickness come over him as the first letters made it obvious who it was.

PHILLIPA.

"Are you our new guide?"

NOT IMPORTANT.

"Are you aware of our thoughts, our discussions?"

It moved quickly to the YES.

"Do you have instructions for us?"

WORK.

"On ourselves?"

It went to the YES.

"What is the link between us?"

TELEPATHY.

"Telepathy between the three of us?"

AS WELL.

"As well as who?" Zuke said.

OTHERS.

"What others?"

PRACTISE.

Warren was unsettled. Both Zuke and Chantal were not concerned that it was Pippa they were supposedly talking to.

Before they had sat round the ouija he had accepted that they were each addressing their own subconscious, that the answers were coming from themselves and not another world, but now that he was supposed to believe that it was Pippa, his Pippa whom they had never known, it was quite unacceptable.

"I am sceptical about all this, Pippa," he said. "I personally need a sign from you, some sort of proof that it is you Pippa Ryder who died less than a week ago."

Even the mention of her death made him shudder, made him aware that up till now he had not faced up to it at all, had not admitted that it had happened. Was it his subconscious trying to get him to accept the fact?

The glass remained quite still in the centre of the table for over a minute, then it started moving slowly, gathering speed as the letters spelt out a message.

GEORGE BIRTHMARK LEFT THIGH.

It was sick.

Sick enough to be coming from him, sick enough to be Zuke playing a joke without even knowing it.

"I knew that already, Pippa. It's personal but not personal enough. George and I used to play squash together. I saw the birthmark in the showers. I need outstanding proof."

The glass vibrated and he felt a frustration coming through. It was a characteristic irritation which Pippa had often displayed when things didn't go right for her and the vibrations through the glass were quite incredible in recalling this mood of hers. It meant that his deepest inner memories were being transmitted to Chantal and Zuke and through them to the glass and back to him, confirming that Pippa could not come up with outstanding proof because Pippa was himself.

Then the glass started to move again, darting from one letter to another as though underlining its message.

GEORGE WILL RING YOU IN TWENTY MINUTES.

They all looked at each other and Zuke, surprised, said, "There isn't a telephone here."

The glass started moving.

PLAYA SOL.

"George is going to ring Warren at the Hotel Playa Sol?" Chantal questioned.

Straight to the YES with such force that their fingers slipped off.

For a distance of several inches the glass had travelled on its own.

"Twenty minutes?" Zuke said, "Can we get down there in time?"

"We must try," Chantal said, getting up, and she turned the glass the right way up.

There were two phone booths in the lounge of the Playa Sol, both were occupied when they walked in.

They sat down in the low red leather chairs, facing the booths, and waited in silence.

He had asked for a sign, a proof, and was now trying to fathom out how a call from George could be explained. If he accepted that he possessed a subconscious telepathic thought process, then it could be that he was right now making contact with George and suggesting the call, but then how had he acquired such a power?

He checked his watch, they had made good time, there were one and a half minutes to go.

He looked across at the booths, both were still occupied and now there was even someone waiting to use whichever phone became free first.

It would seem that Valdez Ortega, Jacinta and even Pippa's contact could soon be dismissed as arrant nonsense.

He checked his watch again and started a private little count down.

Ten, nine, eight, seven . . .

At six he felt a tap on his shoulder. It was the hotel receptionist.

"Señor Ryder? You are wanted on the telephone, at the reception desk."

He exchanged hesitant glances with Chantal and Zuke, who both got up to accompany him to the phone.

He picked up the receiver. "Hallo?"

"Warren, this is George."

He felt his whole being plummet into a void at the sound of the familiar voice.

After preliminary enquiries about his health and his state of mind, George, in an excited tone, told him he had come up with a possible idea for an occult game. It would be called Ouija and be played on a circular board. What had to be worked out was the essential competitive element which would probably be in the area of proving oneself the most psychic person playing the game. The board could be of thick imitation marble plastic and he was sure Warren could come up with all the necessary additions. Warren felt unnerved.

Then George said, "This may sound a bit lunatic, old boy, but I somehow feel I have to tell you, just in case ... I'm still in hospital, ringing from my private room. I sleep a lot, drugs and things, I had a dream this evening, I've just come out of it, which is why I'm calling you now, on impulse, so to speak, but I felt I had to. I dreamt Pippa gave me a message to pass on to you. Are you ready for this, it sounds crazy, but here goes ... when you meet someone called Francisco, his life will be in your hands."

Warren thanked him, made light of the story, said he would work on the "Ouija" idea, meanwhile to rest and try and avoid the nightmares which were bound to invade his mind after the experience he had been through.

He repeated the phone conversation word for word to Chantal and Zuke, and though Chantal thought it proof enough that they were in contact with the supernatural, and Zuke admitted to being pretty well won over, Warren said he would wait to meet this Francisco character and see what happened.

They wandered out into the streets and looked for a bar with pleasant live people to remind themselves what it was to be a member of the human race.

The high-pitched rattle of a waspy engine warned of an oncoming mad teenager on a motorbike disregarding the one way system and everyone's safety. Zuke spun around, cringing, Chantal was instantly irritated and so was Warren. It was the one thing about Spain he really disliked, the constant noise and the total lack of consideration. The natives of Andalusia apparently did not hear noise like others did, it was no concern of theirs. Television sets and transistors and stereos could all be playing loudly in the same room and they would go on talking above the din without noticing. It was aggravating, to say the least, and the small motorbikes without silencers were the worst offenders of all.

They sat down at a terrace café, ordered their own respective drinks and Warren felt a calmness come over him. He respected Chantal because of her seeming aloofness and her self control. He liked Zuke for her mental alertness and her ability to laugh at the quite extraordinary situation they were in.

"Do you think we'll ever need to talk again?" Zuke said. "I mean, will we just be able to transfer our thoughts by telepathy?"

"I hope not," Chantal said. "There are some

thoughts which I would truly prefer to remain private."

"I'm going to try an experiment," Zuke said. "I'm going to guess which man you'd like to go to bed with who passes by here in the next five minutes."

And she checked her watch.

One of the joys of Spain was the late night promenading. It was free theatre of the simplest kind—the "paseo."

They sat in silence, and Warren joined in the game. What man would Chantal choose? He was surprised to find himself observing his own sex from a woman's point of view for the first time. He tried to concentrate through Chantal.

Two youths passed by—tight white jeans, tanned skins, long black hair, they could have been girls, they were beautiful rather than handsome. Would she go for the feminine?

A heavy set German. An idiot in a straw hat. Most individuals were pretty ugly specimens of the human race.

"That one!" Zuke said, pointing to a tanned and arrogant Latin who was licking an ice lolly.

"Absolutely not! I fancied the small man with the hat!" They all laughed.

"Maybe our telepathy is only subconsciously controllable, or not controllable at all, by us?" Zuke suggested.

They had another round of drinks, then Chantal and Zuke played the game with him, choosing the most improbable women on his behalf. Then they decided to call it a day.

As they walked to the car the strident shrill of another motorbike shattered the peace and a boy, revving the engine to an unacceptable crescendo, came towards them caning everyone's ears.

Warren felt a surge of incredible rage. Chantal breathed in and gritted her teeth. Zuke shouted something obscene against the din.

The boy roared past, turned the corner, and suddenly there was a hideous screech of tyres, the shriek of women, the sound of metal scraping brickwork, of glass shattering.

"Oh my God!" Chantal cried out.

Door and shutters opened, lights went on, Warren ran ahead, saw the crash, the disaster. It was not a simple head on collision with a wall—the bike had gone through the plate glass window of a small hardware shop. Jagged pieces of glass hung above the boy's crushed body, his head severed, blood pumping out.

Warren turned round and started back towards Chantal and Zuke to stop them from coming further, from looking, but they were directly behind him, rooted, staring.

Then they looked at each other. It did not have to be said. The death wish. In anger.

They had all wished the boy dead. They had all wished the boy ill, they had all wanted to hurt him, to maim him, to pay for the irritation he was causing.

"Did you want that?" Chantal asked.

"I wanted to hurt him," Warren admitted.

"I wanted him to go right through that particular shop window," Zuke said. "I even imagined the hammers and the saws and the sharp tools . . . I really had it in for him."

"It's a shared power then?"

They didn't want to think about it.

The crowd was now blocking the street completely. Warren, taller than the rest could see three men pulling the blood-soaked body out of the window.

Zuke pressed herself in among the people and recognised someone she knew.

"What happened?"

"Zapped straight into the wall, didn't attempt to take the corner. There was no obstruction. He must have had a blackout, or something funny."

Then a wail rose above the general hubbub, a woman crying, a mother.

"Paco, me Paco . . . Me hijo . . . Paco . . ."

Zuke came out of it all and grabbed Warren's arm, grabbed Chantal's and led them back down the street the way they had come, back towards the bar.

"Did you hear that Warren? The boy's name was Paco."

He shrugged his shoulders, not seeing the significance.

And in a flat voice, drained of feeling, of energy, Chantal said, "Paco is the Spanish diminutive of Francisco."

CHAPTER SIX

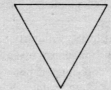

THE Demon Zuke. What had a nice all-American college girl like her done to get involved in all this? What had started as a game to relieve the summer boredom was now turning into something uncontrollable.

Chantal was lying on the sofa sweating and gasping for breath.

She seemed to be in a trance, her eyes fluttering, her lower lip trembling. She was murmuring things, in French, in English, in Spanish, and all that could be done for her was to wipe away the perspiration.

"*Mi amour*," she was now saying, holding onto her hand, very tightly. "You are so sweet. Don't leave me."

Zuke wasn't too sure to whom she was talking. Dabble in the occult and you get nasty surprises.

Warren came in with a cup of tea and suggested she should try and get Chantal to drink it.

Then Chantal quite suddenly sat up, picked at her black silk house gown which was sticking to her body and opened her eyes.

"Are you all right?" Zuke asked.

"Wet through. I'm wet through. I was Valdez Ortega again. Like a dream, yet not. A memory, his memory. Accusations of blasphemy by hypocritical judges. They did not want to understand my book. They did not even want to try. I went mad. I went mad with rage at the injustice of it all. Feel the cushions under me, they're soaking. We'll have to put them outside to dry."

"Are you all right in yourself, physically?"

"I feel fine. It was like a Turkish bath, only with the heat coming out from within. I must have a shower. Come with me, Zuke. I'm too happy being back in the land of the living to risk slipping into the past again. Shake me if I go off again."

After a restless night during which she herself had relived the night of horror with Luis, Zuke had got up early to find Chantal on the sofa where she had obviously gone to sleep, but she had been writhing and perspiring so much that she had called Warren.

Now, in the blue carpeted seclusion and feminine comfort of her bedroom, Chantal suddenly stripped off and stood there quite nude.

What surprised Zuke was that she was so well proportioned, her body so young that she found her not only beautiful, but desirable. She felt she wanted to touch the pert breasts, caress the flat stomach, take her in her arms, embrace her, excite her.

She was thinking like a man.

Chantal went into the bathroom for her shower. She didn't close the door and this intimacy aroused Zuke even more.

She wanted to join her, wanted to undress herself and feel the wet closeness of that pale femininity against her own silky tanned skin.

"Darling," Chantal said, "Could you pass me a clean towel from the airing cupboard, one of the big beach towels?"

Zuke went to get the towel, pleased to be of service, and took it into the steamy bathroom. She had never thought she would find another female body interesting.

"Why don't you have a shower?" Chantal suggested.

Zuke didn't hesitate. She stripped off her T-shirt, her jeans, her briefs. They were the same height, the same build. A perfect couple, the pale one with black hair, the tanned one, blonde.

Chantal looked at her approvingly, studied her with a critical eye. "Have you ever had an affair with a woman?" she asked.

Here it was. Zuke stepped into the shower quickly, checked the water temperature, turned the tap full on. It came down on her, colder than expected, but it was good, just what she needed.

"No!" she shouted. "Have you?"

"Never. I have never had the desire."

Until now? Zuke thought Chantal would stand by watching her, make further suggestions, but she disappeared into her bedroom, and when Zuke got out of the shower to dry herself Chantal was dressed in another house gown, white, her head turbaned in a red kerchief.

Danger over. From whom? Maybe Zuke herself was the protagonist in all this?

They went through the drawing room to the patio and joined Warren, who had prepared breakfast.

"How do you feel?" he asked.

"Very relaxed, well, as though . . ." Chantal hesitated, "As though I had gone through the valley of death and emerged the other side unscathed."

"How about you?"

"I feel fine," Zuke said.

They sat down round the low table and buttered their own toast and drank coffee.

Zuke was pleased it was day time, that the night to come was a good twelve hours away, that they could be together and be individuals doing their own thing.

"He was totally obsessed by the male genitalia," Chantal said suddenly, as though adding her opinion to an argument they might have been having.

"Who?" Zuke asked, astonished.

Chantal looked at her, surprised by the question, then seemed to realise that she had been very deep in her own thoughts. "Marco Duero," she said, coming out of it and looking at each of them. "He was in the service of Tomas de Torquemada, the Inquisitor General in the 1480s."

Zuke glanced at Warren.

He was staring at Chantal, concerned.

"Can you repeat that name?"

"Marco Duero."

Zuke was baffled, it was as though she had missed out on something, as though Chantal's imagined argument had taken place without her hearing it.

Is that what had happened? A telepathic argument between her colleagues from which she had been excluded.

"When did you first hear of Duero?" Warren asked.

"I'm not sure," Chantal said, "I'm not sure I've ever heard of him before, I'm not even sure why I said what I said. In fact, I don't think *I* said anything. It was Valdez talking. Valdez talking in my head."

She stood up and walked to the edge of the pool, stared at the water, turned and came back to sit down.

"My thoughts are very jumbled. It's as though a whole lifetime of information had suddenly been crammed into my mind. For instance, I remember inflicting pain on young men, and enjoying it."

She looked up, wide eyed, and for a moment her innocent smile registered anguish. "But it wasn't me. I was a priest."

Warren now stood up, breathed in slowly, exhaled slowly. Since Zuke had last seen him, since Jacinta's death, his wife's death, he had changed. From a lively, carefree, fun loving character he had become pensive, troubled, afraid.

"I had a dream last night," he said, "A nightmare. A psychic experience perhaps. I'm not sure what it was, but I went back in time, right back and was witness at some poor old man's

execution. I too was a priest, in a black soutane, I wore a black cap and my victim on the
rack was surrounded by four inquisitors wearing cowls. They were like members of the Ku
Klux Klan."

"The Inquisition," Chantal confirmed. "It
must be something to do with Valdez."

"But Valdez lived at the turn of the century," Zuke said, "The Inquisition was in the
fifteenth, surely?"

"Shall we ask the ouija?" Chantal proposed.

"No," Warren said firmly. "I think that before we experiment any further together, we
should sort ourselves out individually." He
then took another deep breath and looking at
both of them tried a brave smile.

"I read the Valdez book right through in the
early hours of this morning, and I've come to
the conclusion, I have been *forced* to the conclusion, that we are dealing with the supernatural and believe that we have triggered off
something unexplainable, a force which is interested in us, but not necessarily for our benefit. Which is why we should tread very
carefully."

"What are you suggesting we should do?"

"Work on ourselves by ourselves till we
come up with something which makes sense
within the new context we're involved in. For
myself I intend going for a walk in the hills

where I can be quite alone. You, Zuke, should also read through the book, see if anything strikes a personal cord."

"Can I stay here?" Chantal asked. "I have so many things to do in the house."

"I think we must all do whatever we feel like doing. I'm only making a suggestion. What I want to find out is whether I can get through a day without something unusual taking place, and whether I am still in control of my own thoughts and actions."

Zuke decided to go to the beach. She hadn't been to the beach since before the toy fair and wanted to get out of the house. She wanted to read the book but was also a little frightened to do so alone. The beach would therefore be an ideal place as she would be surrounded by people but not connected with them.

She walked all the way, deliberately taking her time, by way of Puerto Lucena's main street with its boutiques and tourist shops, seeing familiar faces, friends, acquaintances, some to whom she talked, others to whom she just smiled and waved.

On reaching the road leading down to the beach, she took off her sandals, enjoying the simple sensation of freedom, but when she reached the sand at the bottom she had to sprint quickly to the sea because it was so hot.

She had planned her day, a holiday it would be, with the luxury of a *tombona* mattress, a beach umbrella, and lunch at her favourite *merendero* snack bar.

Nothing had changed, there were just as many people as before, just as many children, topless women, oggling men.

She surveyed the familiar scene as she placed Chantal's black beach towel on the faded mattress and applied Chantal's expensive sun cream down the length of her legs, along her arms, round her shoulders, and patted her face.

Sitting down, she took off her top and massaged cream well into her breasts, smiling at two young men who were staring at her impudently, which was of course flattering.

If it excited them to see a pair of whiter boobs, then good luck to them. Besides, they were both quite handsome, perhaps too handsome, for one of them reminded her of Munich Adonis.

That had been a farce.

A humiliation?

She had been ditched by this fair youth from Munich after a pretty tawdry affair based on hash and guitar playing and his adoration for his own blue eyes, which she had gone along with till he'd started on the adoration of his own fair hair, after the haircut she'd given him.

A slight case of narcissism, that one.

She hadn't fought back. How the hell do you fight narcissism? First you love him because of his physique, then you find he's having an affair with the same person. She'd lost respect the moment she'd found him in the bathroom adoring his own lingam.

"Can I help?" she'd asked.

That was a laugh. And he'd slammed the door in her face. He should have locked it in the first place.

She lay back now, closed her eyes and felt the sun pleasantly toasting her. Was there any better way of spending a day, a lifetime? She had forgotten that this was why she was still in Puerto Lucena.

As her skin started tingling and it became too hot, she imagined plunging into the sea but waited masochistically till she was really sweating, then sat up, clipped on her top and ran into the water.

It was unbelievably refreshing. To dive under in that clear blue water, to open one's eyes and look at the marvels way below the sea bed, the myriad tiny fish darting from the threat of her shadow, the black rocks, the green weeds, the turquoise stones. She floated on her back, duck dived, butterflied back to the beach and lay down again.

Her two male admirers were still there, playing chess on a small board.

She picked up her book, the Valdez Ortega horror, wrapped for her in paper and plastic by the meticulous Chantal.

She felt relaxed enough now to study it with some detachment. This was the right place to read it, with enough diversions to lighten any unpleasant surprises.

She studied the first page, the list of contents.

Oneiromancy—Divination of dreams.
Polypsychism—Mental images perceived through the psyche.
Aethrobacy—The phenomenon of levitation.
Clairaudience—The unheard sound.
Phantasmas—Apparitions in a crisis.
Metempsychosis—Transmigration of souls from the dead to the living.

She decided to read the chapter on metempsychosis again, the passage that had unsettled her so, hardly ten days ago. *"When the character Jacinta in the novel that caused my ignominy . . . transmigrated her soul . . . not a new theory . . ."*

Why had she been so upset? Valdez Ortega had written a novel with a character called Jacinta who had committed suicide, then in real life, a hundred years or so later, a girl of the same name had done just that. The girl had then sent her this very book, none of which could be coincidence, and the anxiety started again.

She put the book down and looked at the people around her. Surely she was safe? How could another world possibly be threatening her?

She turned over a few pages, read the section that had struck Chantal so much, the preparing of the individual to receive another soul.

It was hard to believe. Her anxiety was not well founded in any case. If a spirit from the dead was to enter a body, it was hardly likely to choose her. Chantal was obviously first in line, she had not only experienced these strange visions on her way back from Madrid, and this morning, but had actually flirted with the whole idea, inviting trouble. It was she who so badly wanted to be a medium, and even Warren was a more suitable candidate: for years he'd been dabbling with the occult, and laughing at it.

But he had changed. It was odd that he had so deliberately avoided her these past few days, physically. She was attracted to him, had always been, quite differently from the two boys playing chess. He was immature compared to them. Perhaps it was the mother in her that wanted to fawn on him. It would happen eventually, they couldn't go on living under the same roof and share the same fears without something happening. One day he would need comforting, or she would, and they would hug each other.

It was of course possible that Chantal was after him, that they were already involved and that they had cleverly rid themselves of her for the day.

It wouldn't hurt. It would surprise, but it wouldn't hurt. She liked Chantal too much.

The chess players were looking at her again. Well one of them was, the other was concentrating on the game, on the very few pieces left on the small magnetic board.

She watched him, biting his lower lip, frowning. He picked up a bishop and placed it on another square. His opponent stared down and made a face.

The other sat up and clapped his hands. "Mate!"

They were American, Canadian, maybe English.

Both turned to look at her, and the victor jostled the vanquished, who got up and came directly towards her.

From his sheepishness she guessed that she had been appointed the winner's prize, but that the awkward business of engaging her in conversation was the loser's forfeit.

He had curly black hair held back from his forehead by a tennis player's ribbon. He wore a green swim suit, had a good body with taut muscles, and he was very dark, darker than her, with hairy legs, solid feet, clean carefully cut toenails. He was quite acceptable.

"Your friend won," she said.

"Yes, you."

"What am I supposed to do, lie back and take it?"

"How about a drink first?"

"How about a drink and lunch and a *pedalo* ride first?"

"Right."

His name was John, his friend the winner, Dan. They were Canadians on a month's holiday, students in psychology and anthropology.

They went to the bar. She took her basket with her, holding the book in her hand.

Dan took it from her. He opened it, studied it. "Occult? You into that stuff?"

"Not really. I'm just reading it to please a friend."

He gave it back to her, not interested. She placed it in the basket. As she did so she felt a pang of guilt. "Just reading it to please a friend . . ." It was as though she had been treacherous to a parent, denied a sworn allegiance.

They sat down to lunch with a bottle of

wine—she had two handsome boys all to her-self. It was like the old days when she had first come to Puerto Lucena and lived in a com-mune, before the cost of living had rocketed and she'd had to look for work and all the hippy types had gone.

She'd had a choice of men then. She had a choice now. But something jarred.

The signs were so imperceptible at first that it didn't register immediately. It was in the lift of an eyebrow she was not supposed to see, the gentle touch of a wrist, the fingering of the beads round the masculine neck that triggered the suspicion.

With the wine they dropped the macho act and their pretended interest in women. It sur-prised her, angered her, but she had to go along with it because if she didn't she would find herself alone again with the alternative of read-ing the book or going home, neither of which she wanted to do.

While with them she was living reality, and that's how she wanted it to be for as long as possible.

"Now we're going to take you to see the evil beach!" John said, when they'd finished the meal.

The "evil" beach was a secluded stretch of sand between rocks where the local gays some-times swam in the nude.

The pleasure, she wanted to point out, would no doubt be theirs, not hers.

They got on a *pedalo*, she sat on the paddle cover while they pedalled, and they headed straight for the red rocks and the hidden alcove beyond.

She didn't need the insult of not being wanted, and her anger built up. She had her back to them, was looking straight ahead and could hear them giggling. They had decided that she was fun, and she had accepted them for what they were, and she pretended that she did, but inwardly she was seething. For two men to hire a *pedalo* and go straight to the alcove was telling the world what they were: with a girl in tow they might be thought to be after something else.

Once round the rocks, well away from the main beach, she took off her bikini and dived into the deep clear water. The welcome sensation of total freedom made the situation more acceptable. Who cared?

"Come on you gays, off with them!" She shouted.

They did not hesitate: they slid into the water. The small limp lengths of pink and white hidden in among the curly black bushes amused her.

They started playing. She couldn't see what went on under the water, but she could imagine. It was a form of sexism and she was an outcast.

Alone, she swam back to the abandoned *pedalo*, climbed aboard, put on her bikini and sat down to dry in the sun.

"I'll race you kids to the beach," she suggested.

It was fair. Alone in the machine she couldn't go too fast.

They were competitive. From her seat above the water she watched them swim. They were both beautiful, the lengths of their bodies stretched to the utmost, they were like Grecian statues, but unfortunately they knew it.

It was a fair distance, and she found the going hard, but they all reached the deserted beach more or less at the same time, the boys exhausted, her own leg muscles aching more than was bearable.

They stood up, hands on hips, panting. They looked good, she was turned on by them because of the sun, the sea salt, the seclusion and the freedom.

"OK," she said, sitting down on the sand. "I want to see you two perform. I want to see what you do to each other."

They were shocked. So far nothing had been said seriously, all had been in jest. She was surprised at herself, but she wanted to see them, she really wanted to see what they did.

"We're not like that," John said touchily.

"Exhibitionists or faggots?"

"Neither, damn it!"

He rushed her, put her down flat on her back, pinned her shoulders against the hot sand and straddled her.

She still had her bikini on and he was limp.

"Women don't interest you," she scoffed.

"They do! They do!" he hissed, and went through the senseless motions of raping her, seized by a frantic need to prove himself.

Then Dan, watching them, started laughing.

"She's right, shmuck face, she's right," he chanted.

John got off her and in tears of rage turned on him.

It was quick, brutal and merciless and it aroused her like nothing else had aroused her before.

John, the stronger of the two, hurled himself at Dan, lunged out with clenched fist, winding him so that as he doubled up in pain the uppercut that followed was fatal.

It was not like the movies. Dan did not recover, did not get up, he fell back on the sand to remain there senseless.

It should have ended there, but John was demented. He looked around the beach with lunatic eyes, saw what he wanted and, ape like, ran to a pile of jetsam washed up against the rocks. He picked up a bottle, held it by the neck and crashed it down on the stones.

Now he returned, mad, frenzied, gripping the jagged pieces of glass, stood over Dan's inert body, reached down to grab the boy's penis and slashed at it wildly, hacking it off.

Blood pumped out onto the sand, John looked at what was in his hand, then turned and stared at her aghast.

"Duero ordered me to do it," he said, pleading innocence, "Marco Duero ordered me to do it . . ."

He then fell to his knees and, sobbing, started to smear himself with his friend's blood.

Zuke watched the ritual. She watched. She could not have hoped for a better afternoon's entertainment.

Then she looked at the sea, realised where she was, who she was. It was the second time it had happened.

Subconsciously, she was obsessed by castration.

CHAPTER SEVEN

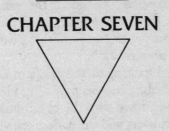

WARREN was not sure. He was not sure at all. His mind was racing, thoughts were invading his imagination so quickly that he could hardly cope.

It could be madness. How did a mad man know he was mad? How did he know whether his actions seemed abnormal to others? How could he tell whether his thoughts were logical or not?

Pippa's death, for example. It had left him empty. Not empty of anything that had been there before, not a feeling of loss, just an awareness that the space reserved for her had always been empty. Or had been for such a long time that he had not even noticed.

When had he ceased loving her? He had never even mourned her.

He walked. It was good, the exercise, the feeling of the limbs moving, it stimulated the thought processes and something would come out of it, an answer.

He liked looking at the range of mountains anyway, feeling he was part of it, climbing up and looking down into the cavernous valley at the pink flowers and the dark green vegetation. He had no idea what they all were, such a city boy was he. He enjoyed the smells, the wild perfumes. Pine he recognised, and rosemary. There was mint, he knew mint. He knew little else.

He picked up a stick and poked at various things, tried to slice a plant but missed. Why the cruel action? An instinctive need to attack and destroy.

Chantal had suggested where he should go, round to the back of the property and up the steep path to the top of the first hill, then follow the cemented irrigation channel which supplied the fields in the valley with ice-cold water flowing down from the mountain sources.

Eventually, she'd told him, it would lead him to a deserted *pueblo*, a few tumbledown houses round a chapel. People had taken refuge there during the civil war but had abandoned them once it was over because there was nothing but a mule track leading to it, and to build a road would have been pointless. There was no farming up on these granite slopes, and certainly no industry.

He was nearly at the top of the mountain now and could look down at the valley below him with its forest of shrub-like trees in the distance. The landscape was dotted with white *cortijos*, the small croft cottages where the grape and olive pickers lived during the harvestings.

Looking back the way he had come he could see Puerto Lucena stretching along the coast, covering quite an area. The Hotel Playa Sol was easily recognisable by its size; the few high rise buildings spoilt what otherwise would be quite a pleasantly laid-out town.

The road up to Chantal's village was easy to follow, winding its way round one hill, then another. It was Vieja Lucena, where the Moors had built one of the first fortifications when they invaded Spain.

Ahead he spotted something white caught in the main stream of the water channel. He thought it was a piece of cloth till he got closer, then it looked more like a drowned animal, a rabbit maybe, a cat, a bird perhaps, a white owl, though it had too much flesh on it to be a bird.

He was standing over it before he realised

what he was staring at and stepped back in horror.

It was a human hand, severed just above the wrist.

The hand, fleshy, translucent, soft, puffed with water, was clenched, the nails yellow. There were several tendons and nerves floating loose and he could see the bones where it had been hacked off from the arm.

It was repulsive and quite sickening, and he moved away from it quickly.

An accident? A man losing a hand up here in the hills? How? The revolting image so unsettled him that he decided to move away from the water channel and keep to the mule track, just in case another limb should come floating down.

Then he heard chanting and, round the slope of the mountain, on the very path he was walking, came a strange procession of local villagers dressed as though for a pageant.

Perhaps it was a Saint's Day, and this one of the many pilgrimages to one of the mountain sanctuaries?

He stepped off the track to let them pass. A leading choir boy was holding a cross aloft, followed by several older men dressed in long white, black and scarlet robes, wearing cowls over their heads, awe inspiring, dauntingly medieval.

Behind them, roped together, were ten or so bare footed individuals wearing yellow sackcloth tunics on which were sewn various Christian symbols. Some had red crosses on their backs and fronts, others a half cross, others still flames pointing downwards, some with flames pointing upwards. Each carried a green candle and stared ahead or up at the sky as though crazed, waiting for a sign from . . . God?

The chanters followed, peasants dressed poorly in threadbare garments. It was an odd sight and he stood there watching them, smiling as a tourist smiles at the quaint customs of another country, when a mule came round the slope dragging two heavy sacks tied to the end of a long rope.

When it passed him and he looked down, he saw that they were not sacks, but two corpses hideously bruised and bleeding, tied by the ankles, a woman and a man, naked, their hands tied above their heads, their arms dragging, except the man had no hands, just two severed stumps.

"Heretics!" he whispered to himself.

The satisfaction he felt at the fearful sight brought him to his senses. The feeling that what he was looking at was divinely right was astonishing. Then he realised that he was standing quite alone, that the chanting had stopped, that there was no evidence at all that the procession had passed.

He had looked up at the fanatical expressions, the pained faces, the martyred grimaces, he had even looked up at the leading boy carrying the cross.

The ghosts had been taller than him, for they had been ghosts, he was sure, and he had been a small boy observing them.

"The *Sanbenitos*," he said to himself, remembering.

They were the yellow sackcloth tunics, the garments of shame. If he followed the procession now he would see the burning, for those with the flames pointing upwards would be burnt alive, and those with flames pointing downwards would be strangled at the stake because they had confessed at the eleventh hour.

The *auto-da-fé*.

What had the Inquisition to do with him?

He turned on his heels and started down the mule track, then ran along the irrigation channel as fast as he could.

By the time he reached Chantal's villa he realised that he was in a terrible state of nerves. Though he knew that they could not have been real, the images of the severed hand and those mutilated bodies being dragged by the mule had been very disturbing.

He paused outside the gate to regain his

breath, determined not to look as drained as he felt, and when he went up the entrance steps, walked through the hallway and into the living room, he guessed that he had not been the only one to go through a horrendous experience.

Zuke was sitting on the edge of the sofa, her hands covering her face, Chantal massaging her neck.

Chantal told him what had happened to her. Zuke was unable to speak for herself, did not even want to hear it being recounted.

"Why are you back so soon?" she asked.

He told her what he had seen.

"We have to consult the ouija," Chantal said. "It will be the only way that we can learn what is happening, quickly and directly. I know you are reluctant, I know you are against it, but by now you must admit it is at least a means of finding out what forces are working on us."

"Does Zuke want to do the ouija?"

"Zuke wants to be free of whatever has entered her mind."

Warren shrugged his shoulders.

"I have to confess something," Chantal then said. "I have been doing the ouija alone."

"With what results?"

"A message came to me, not through the glass, but into my mind. It could have been imagined, but remembering what Valdez said in his book about always being open to the receiving of esoteric signals, that communication with the dead is never complicated . . . it could have been a message from Jacques."

"Your late husband?"

"When I sat down alone at the table this afternoon, I was thinking of him, I was thinking that perhaps if I tried to contact only him he would help me. I sat with my finger on the glass, it did not move, but I heard his voice in the depths of my mind, it felt like a warning which was not coming from him alone. It came from Carlos too, Luis and . . . Pippa. All those with whose deaths we have been involved."

At times Chantal talked like some old-maid medium, like a clairvoyant in Clapham sitting in a front room surrounded by aspidistras and smelly cats.

"I would like us to sit round the ouija and concentrate very hard on friends and relations who have died and try and summon their spirits in order to get an explanation of what is happening from them. Will you join me? I need your energy to move the glass. I am sure that only good can come out of it."

They waited till it was dark, sitting on the patio in silence drinking iced coffee, each with their own thoughts again.

Zuke was more relaxed now, could talk of what had happened. The Guardia Civil had ap-

parently questioned her about the beach tragedy. She had made a statement and was now
worried that a connection would be made between what had happened today and Luis's
suicide. If the authorities were thorough, sus-
picions would be aroused about Jacinta's death
and Carlos's in Madrid. On the other hand, as
Chantal kept repeating, because they were in
Spain, because the Press did not hunger for
sensationalism as it did in other countries, because they were still in a small resort which
might not want bad publicity, they could escape unscathed.

"It's not the public I'm afraid of," Zuke said.
"It's the unexplainable that keeps on happening. We're cursed!"

"Do you really feel that we are, that whatever it is motivating all this is evil and against
us?" Chantal asked. "I don't, you see. I feel
we're definitely being used and not necessarily
to our disadvantage. That's why I want to contact my Jacques."

Then Zuke suddenly got up and suggested
they should get on with it, she suggested that
they should close all the doors and windows,
switch off the electricity, light two or three
candles and concentrate on the ouija till they
got satisfaction.

And in this mood of determination, they sat

round the marble table and placed their fingers on an upturned glass.

"I am calling on Jacques Daubigny. *Jacques, es tu la?*" Chantal chanted.

There was a terrifying naivety about her attitude which Warren found irritating.

They waited. They waited longer than they had waited before, and Chantal repeated the question not once but four times. Still nothing happened.

"There's clearly no one there," Zuke said. "I've always felt some vibrations, however weak, before."

"Has the contact gone then?" Warren questioned.

"It can't have done."

"Luis are you there?" Zuke tried.

Nothing.

"Perhaps we were wrong to switch off the electricity, perhaps a current in the house helps?" Warren said.

"Let's switch on then. Switch on and open the windows."

He helped Zuke open the doors and all the windows as before while Chantal turned on the mains switch.

They sat down again, this time with light coming from a small lamp in the corner.

They each placed their fingers on the glass and waited.

"Is anyone there?" Warren asked, somehow happier.

If they needed the electricity switched on then they were not dealing with the supernatural. They were dealing with a phenomenon, with something pretty odd, but it would at least be of this earth.

But the glass did not move.

"What is the matter?" Chantal asked impatiently, even hurt. "Jacques, I want to talk to you, I want your help. I want an explanation. Jacques, are you there?"

"Perhaps we're all too tense, too anxious," Warren said. "Maybe we should leave it for a while, go outside, have a drink and relax. We may be pressing too hard and putting up some sort of block."

Chantal said nothing, but stood up, turned the glass the right way up, supposedly releasing any spirit that might have been near at hand, and led the way to the living room.

Warren was standing at the edge of the pool sipping a Sangria the girls had made. Zuke was lying on the patio couch, Chantal sitting in a deck chair, when they all heard a shattering crash from inside the house.

They ran in, Chantal switching on all the lights.

In the dining room they found that the heavy

circular marble ouija table had been flung
across the room to land on the dresser, break-
ing every piece of Chantal's dinner service, all
her cups, saucers, glasses, bowls, her priceless
Hispano Moresque plates.

The marble top was intact, resting against
the splintered woodwork, but somehow vibrant.

As Warren stared at the disaster, Zuke and
Chantal just behind him, he saw the marble
table top move.

Slowly it rolled of its own volition, crushing
the broken pieces of glass and porcelain on the
hard tiles in its way. It rolled clear of the de-
bris then started rotating. Warren thought he
was watching a giant coin gathering momentum again after having spun itself flat. The
huge marble wheel seemed to waltz to life on
its outer rim, lift off, steady itself on its edge,
fall again, pick up the energy and turn.

It gathered speed, it whirred like a top, gy-
rated with such power that all that could be
seen was a translucent globe shimmering in
the middle of the room.

Then it started towards them. In its path was
a glass coffee table, a lampstand, a miniature
chair.

It cut right through them, fracturing the table and showering the room with fragmented
glass, it buckled the brass lampstand, hurling

pieces to left and right, it ground the miniature chair to sawdust and still came on.

It was Chantal who screamed. It was she who used their voices, their energy, their united psychic power to halt it.

It was not just a scream, it was a fearful bellow, an inhuman cry that echoed and re-echoed into the very heart of the vibrating sphere, and its pace slowed down as though the current had been turned off. It waltzed again, became a table top again, faltered, then spun itself flat to the ground like a huge discarded discus.

All three, at the same time, realised that verbal communication between them was not necessary. They were thinking as one. They knew instantly what they had to do.

Zuke collected the pedestal base from the littered corner and put it down in its place, Chantal and Warren lifted the heavy marble top and lowered it into position only to realise as they were doing so that it was unbelievably hot.

Warren got three chairs while Chantal fetched a tumbler from the kitchen, and all three sat down to place their finger tips on the upturned base.

This time there was no waiting.

The message reached the inner depths of their minds without being spelt out.

YOU ARE MINE. ONLY MINE. NO HELP CAN COME FROM OTHERS.

ARMANDO VALDEZ ORTEGA.

Warren felt himself come out of it, felt himself being released from the grip of whatever power Valdez had over him, over his mind. It was a sense of relief, of light headedness.

"Then you must answer our questions!" Chantal shouted.

Warren looked across at her, at Zuke. Neither had their fingers on the glass but simply rested the flat of their hands on the warm surface of the marble.

"What was that demonstration? That performance? That manifestation?" Chantal asked. She seemed outraged by the damage caused.

IT WAS TO PROVE TO YOU THAT I EXIST.

The words did not sound in his head, he heard them mentally as though a receiver were speaking in the very centre of his brain.

"Who are you, what are you and what are you doing to us?"

READ AND FIND AND FIND . . .

An electric current passed over the surface of the marble which made them all lift their hands off. It was a mild shock, like static electricity, and when they touched the table again it felt dead.

"Read and find and find . . . ?" Zuke repeated looking at them. "Is that what you got?"

"That is exactly what I got," Chantal said.

"Me too," Warren confirmed. "So what do we do?"

"Study the book. Perhaps there are clues in it to something we've missed?" Zuke suggested.

She made it sound like a whodunnit, an occult mystery. A spirit was playing games and he did not know what part he had been cast in.

He was good at games, however, he invented them. Detection, research, tracking down was his field. It was a question of organising a system of elimination. Up till now he had not wanted to find out anything, but his attitude was changing.

Chantal and Zuke sat together on the sofa in the sitting room and poured over the *Discourse*. Page by page they went over the subject matter hoping to find something meaningful. He sat alone, a little distance from them, with a pad and pen and started doodling. It helped the mind to work.

Going back to the beginning, the important question was not so much why things were happening, but why things were happening to *them*?

All that they had in common was that they were foreigners in Spain, had no past connection with the country. They were all of different ages, backgrounds, cultures. They had come together because they were all, more or less, interested in the occult: he played games, Chantal was a dabbler, Zuke had an amateur interest. He didn't feel it was that.

Was it then something more basic? Like the table itself? The house? Was it the house which was haunted?

"What was this place before you bought it, Chantal?" he asked.

"An olive oil mill. They used to bring the olives here and crush them. The only old part is the dining room, which was the mill-house."

"Do you know anything about the people who lived here before?"

"No one lived here before. It was just a place of work. It was even open to the four winds."

"Did anyone ever die here?"

"I don't think so, but I don't know."

"What was it before it was a mill?"

"I don't think it was anything. The original building goes back to the seventeenth century."

"Was that still the time of the Inquisition?"

"The Inquisition went on for five hundred years, from the thirteenth to the eighteenth centuries. It must have been."

"Why did I have these visions of the Inquisition? Is it possible that they burnt people at the stake on this site?"

"Perhaps."

"Could it have been a prison, a place of torture?"

"I'm not sure how we could find out."

Find . . . find . . . Jacinta had been a link. The thought was unsettling. That night when he had challenged the ouija, that had been the beginning. Jacinta coming to him as though she had been an offering, which he had dared take.

"What do you know about Jacinta's past?"

"She was born in the village, both her parents were born in the village."

"Can you go further back?"

"Her grandmother is from here as well."

"How did her parents die?"

"Her father was drowned when a fishing boat went down. Her mother died giving her birth."

"The grandmother must remember her own grandparents, that would take us back a few generations."

"Yes, but why?"

"Supposing, just supposing that Jacinta was related to Valdez? Because he comes in here somewhere. He's the key figure."

"My God!" Chantal said suddenly, standing up, "Why didn't we think of it before? That's why she would have had the book."

"Her being related, you mean?"

"The simplest things . . . Communication with the dead is never complicated."

167

* * *

The next morning he went with Chantal to visit the grandmother. They brought her some flowers, and were shown into the dark windowless room in the middle of the house.

They sat on hard chairs, and she offered them a glass of the local wine which was cloudy and potently sweet.

Warren understood little of what she said, but it was clear that Chantal was making general conversation, asking about the family, about their health, about the crops they farmed down in the valley. It was polite, discreet, she handled it well.

Somewhere along the way he heard the grandmother mention the name Ortega. She said it very casually and he watched Chantal check a reaction of victory.

She asked another question and the grandmother spoke more freely, nearly excitedly, then she got up and left the room to fetch something.

"Valdez Ortega was the father of her great grandmother. Four generations back," Chantal said, her eyes bright with anticipation at further discoveries. "She says she has something which might interest us."

The old lady had gone out to the patio and the stable at the back where Jacinta had hung herself. He could see her moving about in the shadows, then she reappeared carrying a metal deeds box.

She placed it on the table, pulled back the rusty catch and opened the creaking lid. The box contained several small leather bound books, a manuscript and a number of letters.

The old woman could not read, papers were foreign to her and she picked up the books with a certain apprehension, handing them to Chantal, who looked through them and handed them to Warren.

They were all copies of the original *Discourse* in Spanish. The original manuscript written in long hand was at the bottom of the box, the letters were tied together with ribbon and there was an illuminated document on parchment written in Latin. He glanced through it and stared with disbelief at the signature and the date.

Marco Duero de Lucena. 1476.

CHAPTER EIGHT

ZUKE was alone in the house.

She had never been alone in the house before. She had been a guest many times, had
slept in both spare rooms, had taken baths in
both bathrooms and cooked in the kitchen, had
swum in the pool and sunbathed in the garden,
but she had never been alone.

Wearing nothing but a near transparent kaftan, she now wandered from room to room,
standing quite still in each of them to get a
feeling of the place for herself.

Chantal had designed the villa for privacy,
using the house itself as a shield from the village, and the sloping garden to hide the pool
from the olive groves beyond.

In her apartment Zuke had privacy in the bathroom and that was about all, the kitchen and bed-sitting room had such large windows that the world itself could look in, and it did, from the high rise opposite.

She went to the kitchen to make herself a cup of coffee, and sauntered out to the pool. She looked back at the house. Aesthetically it was not a masterpiece: additions and terraces were there for a purpose and were architecturally too fussy. She climbed up the steep tiled steps to the flat roof and from there gazed at the unique panorama of the surroundings; the whitewashed houses, the church tower with its bell, the vine slopes to the north, the sparkling sea in the distance. She was standing on the original part, the old mill, and realised that she had actually avoided going in there. Was she then afraid of another manifestation?

She went down the steps and through the French windows into the room. The ouija table was in the corner, a piece of furniture, nothing more.

There was the long refectory table with its pewter candlesticks and the various antique farm implements Chantal had collected and hung on the wall. It was a room she did not much like, a little too obvious, a little too much like a tourist bar, with the old millstone as centre piece and the wooden beams stark against the bright whitewash.

She placed her mug of coffee on the marble table and sat down, her back to the window, facing the room.

Was it haunted? If it was, would she see an apparition now, at eleven-thirty in the morning? She put her hand flat on the cold marble surface. No sensations, no vibrations. In the clear of day all that she had been through was like a dim nightmare.

Some memories were part of her, childhood memories, but not any of the recent past. It could all have been imagined.

She was about to get up, give up and get up and go for a swim, when she sensed something behind her.

It was not a noise, it was not a movement of air, it was simply the feeling of a presence.

She was no longer alone and it frightened her. She did not want to turn and look because she did not want to face the unimaginable.

She closed her eyes for a moment, opened them again and felt the presence move past her, further into the room. There was nothing to see, but she knew it was there, moving along the side of the refectory table, stopping now and turning to face her.

She looked. There was nothing to see. Yet it was there.

"Who are you?" she asked in the terrible silence.

No answer. No sound. The presence moved on, turned its back on her and went out of the far door.

Should she follow? She was afraid of doing so because of the dark hallway between the dining room and the kitchen. She could be trapped there.

She watched the doorway, stared at the obscurity beyond it, such a small area. The light switch was immediately to the right.

The presence was drawing her, beckoning her, daring her. What was she so frightened of then, death? Pain? She was afraid of being afraid, of suffering a shock, of seeing something so hideous that her heart would stop beating.

But she stood up. She walked slowly towards the door, two steps up to the new tiles, five steps and she would be in the sunny kitchen.

Was it a test of bravery? Did the presence know what it was asking of her? She moved forward, up on the first step, the second. She was level with it and very close.

It was there. It could reach out and touch her if it wanted to. She had to go on, she had to, but would she pass through it?

Was that what it wanted? For her to pass through it? She closed her eyes and threw herself forward. She was in the kitchen so quickly she couldn't believe it, the brightness, the sunshine, the copper pans, the polished sink.

She turned and looked back and saw it: a silhouette against the dim light coming from the dining room, framed in the doorway, very clear, very solid.

"Zuke?"

It was Warren.

"Jesus!" she said, "Are you alive?"

"I hope so. Why?"

"Oh . . . I don't know. Imagination, who can tell?"

Chantal was behind him. They came into the kitchen and placed a heavy metal box on the table.

"What's that?"

"Hopefully, everything explained. Jacinta's great, great, great grandfather, six generations back anyway, was Valdez Ortega. It's all here, her grandmother has allowed us to go through it all."

Zuke was suddenly aware that she was trembling.

"Are you all right?" Chantal asked, "You look ashen."

"There was something here."

And she told then what had happened, or rather what had not happened.

"Was it Jacinta, do you think?" Warren

asked. "We could have disturbed something with our prying."

"No, it was male." She hadn't thought of it at the time, but somehow had known the presence was male.

"Was it evil?"

"Not particularly. I think it wanted something from me."

"Well, a male would," Warren said, looking her over.

It was the first time since his return from London that he had either looked at her that way, or even made a humorous remark. It was a relief. It was human.

"We've got four copies of Valdez's book here, his original manuscript, a whole lot of letters and an illuminated parchment signed by Duero," Chantal said, opening the box and taking some of the papers out. "I think we should go outside on the patio and read through everything till we find something significant."

It was a warm windless day, they sat under the algarrobo tree, each with pen, paper and necessary reference books to work silently and with determination.

Warren was translating the Latin document signed by Marco Duero, Chantal was sorting out the letters, Zuke was comparing the Spanish text of Valdez's books with the English translation, together with the handwritten manuscript, looking for additions or discrepancies.

"Here's something," Chantal said after a while, holding up one of the letters.

"I'll translate it very loosely . . . It's a copy of a letter from Valdez to his wife, written from Madrid, presumably to London, dated 12 July 1872.

Querida . . . I believe that last night I made contact with my guide. With a candle between myself and the mirror, that is between myself and my own reflection, I concentrated for two hours before an ectoplasm materialised. It formed behind me, behind my reflection, and took the shape of my aura. It was very faint, like curling smoke from a tobacco pipe. It was Marco Duero. I heard him clearly, within my inner ear, and he told me that I was now ready for metempsychosis. I am to be used for his reincarnation and he has assured me that once we are one, I will have psychic powers enabling me to prove my theories to my adversaries. When I die, when Duero and I die, we will re-enter the world in another being thus perpetuating ourselves for ever. The training was at times distasteful, but I have overcome my fears. Humanity can only survive the passage of

time if the mysteries of the afterlife are un-
veiled. I will devote myself to this unveiling,
even at the risk of eternal damnation."

Zuke was watching Chantal as she read. She
had paled, she had gone quite white.

"We will re-enter the world through another
being . . ." Chantal repeated. "The training was
at times distasteful." She looked up. "Would
you say that what we have been through was
distasteful?"

"Yes," Zuke said. "Luis and the blood-
letting on the beach have been just that. Distasteful to witness, distasteful to have wished
it."

"What are the other letters?" Warren asked.

"Mainly to his lawyer about the clearing of
his name. Explanations of what he meant, how
he was misunderstood." She picked up another
letter. "This one is from Carabanchel, the
prison, dated 7 October 1902 . . .

My dear Son.

Sentence has now been passed and I am to
face the garotte next Wednesday at dawn.
Apart from the pain I fear, as anyone fears
pain, I am not frightened of death, as you
well know. Wednesday will mark a day of
advancement for me for once in limbo I will
contact you. Failing this I will search and

choose another suitable being. I regret that you never approved of my work and at times believed me insane, but I chose to walk a lonely path of experimentation and in the depth of my heart forgive you misunderstanding my aims. In time I will be proved right. In time you will be proud to bear the name which you so hurtfully disowned . . . I have but one request and that is for you to keep intact the contents of the box I leave behind me, my only possessions after a lifetime on this earth."

"Did he ever make contact with his son, I wonder?" Warren said, "through the ouija or any other means?"

"I don't think he did," Chantal said, "I don't exactly know why, but I feel his family never took an interest in him once he was gone, and that Jacinta was the first with whom he *could* communicate."

Zuke thought the same. It was not that she agreed with Chantal, it was that she somehow knew that this was the truth. It was surprising that Warren had no inkling of this.

"What is the parchment about?" she asked him.

"It's a prayer. I don't know what sort of prayer, but that's what it must be. It ends *dominus vobiscum, amen.*"

"So though it doesn't mean anything in it-self, the fact that a parchment signed by Duero is in the box suggests a psychometric contact between him and Valdez?" Zuke suggested.

Both Chantal and Warren agreed.

"Which leaves us where? Are we involved because we consulted the ouija with Jacinta or because we consulted it here, on Duero's and Valdez's territory?"

"I think that that is the accident," Warren said, "Jacinta was Valdez, Valdez was Duero. We're dealing with this awful experiment in metempsychosis."

"Are we then being entered by all three?" Zuke asked. It was a fearful idea but made ter-rible sense.

"Possibly. But which one is being entered by whom?"

"Who do you feel you are, Zuke?" Chantal asked.

"I don't know," she said guardedly. "I've sensed no connection with Valdez like you have. You relived the garotte, which must be him. I would say Duero, because of that obsession."

"Just that?"

"It's enough, isn't it? I also felt I was trans-ferring psychic thoughts to other people, spe-cially the boys on the beach. I felt they were being motivated by me, or rather by Duero through me. On the other hand I also feel more sexually orientated, randier to put it simply, and that comes from Jacinta."

"Jacinta wasn't randy!" Chantal exclaimed, laughing at the idea.

"Oh I think she was. Going to Warren's room, flirting with him like she did."

"She wasn't a flirt!"

"I think she was. I think she was a 'butter wouldn't melt in her mouth' little girl."

"What about you, Warren?"

"Duero. Very strong. The ghosts I saw up on the hills could only be his memories. But I'm not sure this theory works. Pippa, after all, was affected somehow by Jacinta's spirit. She mentioned her name to George before rushing to the tube station and hurling herself in front of the train."

"Jacinta through you? Perhaps they're all three trying at once and don't know who to choose?"

"Perhaps," Zuke offered. "We still have a chance, then."

"Of escape?"

"Why not? Maybe they're not that strong . . . yet."

"Then perhaps we should separate again, while the going's good?"

"Escape to where?" Chantal queried a little mockingly.

181

Zuke caught Warren's eye.

The same thought had occurred to him, she was sure. Chantal, unlike him and herself, wanted the metempsychosis to take place, wanted to experience more psychic phenomena. Of the three of them Chantal could well be the motivating force for everything that had happened, could already have been entered by Valdez or Duero, or Jacinta.

"I would like to put it to the vote," Warren said, "That we separate to study ourselves individually."

"For how long?" Chantal asked.

"Just a few hours."

He was going to run away, Zuke knew it, he was creating an excuse to leave them.

"You're afraid, Warren," Chantal said. "And you're preparing yourself an escape route. You see, *mon cher*, we can no longer hide anything from each other, our telepathic communication has already started solidifying. Zuke knew what you were thinking, and I can tell you both that I know you suspect me of wanting to put my head in the lion's mouth. Well, you're right. But if you leave me you will be haunted. I believe the process of metempsychosis has already started and that there is little we can do but accept it and, indeed, enjoy it. After all, if it works, does it not mean a form of invincibility, of perpetuity, of divinity?"

She was mad, Zuke thought. Perhaps she had always been mad. And Chantal turned and smiled at her.

"If I am mad, then so are you. But the difference between us for the moment is that I am admitting my madness, whereas you are still fighting yours."

Not much else of value could be gathered from the Valdez letters, his book or manuscript. Running to over three hundred pages in the Spanish original, and just under in the English, there were the same number of chapters and all the headings were similar.

"Find . . . find . . ." The ouija had dictated. Had they found?

They had a silent lunch together, Warren hardly touching his food. Chantal had been right in saying there was no getting away, they were caught in the ouija net which extended, for all they knew, over the whole globe, over the whole universe, and escaping from it would be like trying to escape from himself.

After the meal he went to lie down in his room. It was on the western side of the house, cool and sunless until evening when the low window afforded a view of the distant hills and the red sunset reflected on the sea.

At three in the afternoon, however, it was in the shadows and peaceful. Warren lay on top of the bed with nothing on but his cotton trousers, and looked at his bare feet. They were brown now, sun-tanned, pleasing, his toe nails comparatively white. He had long feet and putting them together reminded him of a sculptured Christ's feet nailed to the cross, or feet at the end of a rack to be dismembered like that hand and wrist in the water.

He closed his eyes and placed his hands under his head and breathed in slowly, deliberately. He stretched. He hadn't stretched for years it seemed, had not relaxed, had not given himself time to do so. Ever since leaving school he had been on the go, competing in the great commercial world for a place of recognition, for money.

School . . . He went back to that wretched playground where it always seemed to be raining, with the red brick wall and the smelly latrines. He was there now, in his imagination, very clearly, and surprisingly it was bathed in sunshine and quite deserted. It was as though he was actually there on a hot August afternoon during the summer holidays, for he noticed changes. The woodwork round the schoolroom windows had been painted a bright blue, there were funny paintings on the cement, a mural on the latrine wall, and the latrine had bright painted doors now.

He moved down the street, along the suburban avenue with its semis on either side. He hadn't been down it since he was ten, since they had moved to the country. Numbers seven, nine, eleven, thirteen. Number nine had new windows, and a new garage. The trees were much thicker, there was more foliage. The cars were new, too. This was no memory but a visit, as though he were there now. There were new number plates, two Metros, a Citroën Visa, and at the end of the road a block of flats which had not been there in his schooldays.

Was he there now? He nearly opened his eyes, but decided not to.

He thought of his parents and made a conscious effort to imagine himself in their house, in the small Berkshire village. He sped across the bridge spanning the Thames, the islands on the left crowded with overgrown willows, their roots holding the banks together, past the water mill, the estate to the right with sand coloured brickwork, mock Georgian windows—an expensive, exclusive estate. He hadn't been there for four months. He passed the Red Lion on the right, the Vicarage on the left, the sub-post office which was closed.

Thursday, early closing. Was he there then? He approached his parents' cottage with its low brick wall, the roof once thatched now tiled. He went up the brick footpath past his father's roses in the front garden. They were out in bloom under the wild cherry tree.

The door was painted white with the black horse-shoe knocker. He was about to press the bell, to bang the knocker, but instead went through. He just went through.

He was in the narrow hallway now with its fitted beige carpet, the narrow stairs immediately to the left, the living room to the right. No one was there. Clean, spotless, it was ready for the unexpected visitors who never came; the corner cupboard with the sherry, the corner bookshelf with the Staffordshire china. On the chimney piece was a printed invitation.

"At Home. Roger and Harriet. 6:30. 4th September."

He was actually there. He looked down at his feet, but could only see the pattern of the carpet.

He went into the dining area with its hatch through to the kitchen. The new sliding double-glazed windows, quite ugly, were open, and his father was out there in his shirt sleeves mowing the lawn, pipe in his mouth, soundless.

There was no noise.

He moved to the kitchen. His mother was there, washing up after lunch, with her apron on, her white hair recently permed and tinted blue, wearing new glasses. He had not seen them, she had told him about them at Pippa's funeral.

Quite suddenly she turned, very abruptly, nearly dropping the dish she was wiping dry, and she looked straight at him, her face expressing horror.

"Mother?" he said quietly.

She put the dish down, lifted her rubber gloved hand quickly to her heart and leaned against the sink. She puffed out her cheeks and smiled at herself, then went out of the back door to the garden to breathe more deeply.

"You all right dear?"

He didn't hear his father, the words were mouthed, he understood them, but he did not hear them.

"I had an awful fright. I thought I saw Warren coming into the kitchen behind me."

"You must stop worrying about him . . ."

Had she been worrying about him? He had been very distant at the funeral, not wanting any help, or sympathy from anyone. They had come to the flat afterwards and she had wanted to tidy up and he had fiercely rejected her help. She had understood, but all the same had been hurt because she was the only person he could turn to, having lost the only other woman in his life.

He was in the flat now. In his London flat. Musty, airless, silent, just as he had left it, except for the letters neatly arranged on the kitchen table by Iris who lived above, to whom he had given the key.

He went to look at the plants, the earth in the pots was not dry, she had come to water them as she had promised.

He went along the line of books, the stack of games, his games, his inventions, his creations. Medium, The Swift Tarots. It had all started there.

He went into the bedroom, looked at the double bed stripped as he had stripped it, stuffing the dirty sheets into the laundry basket.

Could he look into the laundry basket? Could he lift the cover? He went into the bathroom, it glowed with a blue light. He did not have to switch on the electricity. The one room without windows, the one place where he would need to use artificial light glowed phosphorescently.

He lifted the lid of the laundry basket. The sheets were still there, the ones that George and Pippa had slept in. He replaced the lid, returned to the kitchen, picked up each letter to study the envelopes. Mostly bills, of course, a card from a friend in Australia who hadn't heard the news, and letters of condolence he did not want to read. He thought of opening them, but it would be unfair to Iris. What would she think if she found the place he had entrusted to her disturbed? He replaced them as he had found them.

Were ghosts people like himself, live people haunting the living? He could go and see George. He could go and see anyone he chose, perhaps. Was this astral projection, was this a form of psychic power he had gained?

He went to see George. He went to St. Stephen's Hospital, Santo Estefano. The private wards were on the third floor. He was there straight away with no effort or as much effort as it takes the imagination to travel fifty miles.

He was there, standing at the foot of the bed, but George was no longer in it. Another patient, a woman, staring at him but not seeing.

Where would George be? Back home, convalescing?

Maidenhead, the country house, the six roomed country house. He was there, on the gravel driveway looking at George's BMW and his wife's Mini parked in the open double garages.

Then the surprise. He was inside the house but could not turn left, he could not go left into the room he knew to be the study. He could go straight on, into the living room and through to the back, he could go into the dining room, into the kitchen, but he was unable to go into a room he had never visited and unable to go upstairs.

As he placed his foot on the first step it seemed to no longer exist, a wall of greyish matter clouded his vision, and it felt oppressive.

Was it that in astral projection you could only go where you had already been before?

George was out in the garden, sitting in a deck chair, reading the paper.

He could practise on George, he could find out what powers he had on human beings. George owed him a favour or two.

He walked up behind him, gripped the top of the newspaper and tore it out of his hands.

George was amazed.

He bunched it up, screwed up the whole newspaper then kicked it across the lawn.

George got slowly to his feet, turned, stared straight at him, but could not see him, though it was obvious that he could see something, a shape, an ectoplasm perhaps.

He had not looked at himself in the mirror.

"Jean!" George shouted. His voice was strangled, frightened. "Jean!"

Jean came out, like his mother, wearing an apron, wiping her hands, the domestic housewife forever cleaning.

"What's the matter, darling?"

"Nothing . . . nothing. I just . . ."

"What's the newspaper doing like that?"

"I don't know . . . it was like a poltergeist."

So that is what he was like. He went back to the drawing room, pastel shades of pink everywhere, the cushions, the wallpaper, the carpet. He looked at the framed photographs on the piano, opened the keyboard lid and touched a few notes.

He struck a chord. A mischievous spirit!

He went over to the ornate mirror which was not an antique but a reproduction and stood in front of it and looked.

It was frightening. There was no reflection, but a movement, hardly discernible, like the faint vapour caused by heat on the surface of a car bonnet, or a road, a mirage, a kink in the atmosphere, a presence.

Where had he always wanted to go, but never been?

The art department of Garnet's, the rival games people to see what his opposite number was doing.

He was there, but only outside the factory, in the car park looking at the portacabins which they used as design studios. As soon as he stepped beyond a certain area, all clouded, it just no longer existed. He had been there once after a meeting of the Toy Manufacturers' Federation when he had given his competitor a lift back.

He opened his eyes. His feet were at the end

of the bed, his hands behind his head. A dream or reality?

Could he then go anywhere he had been before?

He thought hard. Holidays, long ago as a child, foreign countries. France, Brittany. He was there, along a seashore he did not remember. He had been there with his parents, had played in the rock pools looking for crabs, but the line of houses and the immense space of sand were familiar. The beach itself was crowded, August, holidays. He made a conscious effort to move. Thought of Paris, was there near Notre Dame. He moved swiftly across a bridge, as swiftly as the fast moving traffic. It was not that familiar. The Paris he knew was the Champs-Elysées, the Moulin Rouge, the Hotel Trianon during the Toy Fair of three years back with George—hungry for girls, always hungry for girls. They had strolled the streets, the Rue Godot de Mauroy, accosting the tarts, he remembered that, but he wasn't there now. He was on the left bank. It was an unfamiliar street off Boulevard Saint Germain. He walked along the crowded pavement. Paris was hot in August, there were not many people, tourists mainly. He brushed against some of them deliberately, they turned, dusting their jackets, one woman visibly shivering and stopping to look back.

A manifestation on a Paris boulevard. He was being drawn to an area, he felt it, this was not wishful thinking, he was no longer in control of the projection. He looked up at the enamel name plate, white on blue. Rue Monge. A little way along on the left there were two ambulances and police cars, their bright blue lights flashing the message of emergency.

It was to this that he was being drawn. A door was open, a doorway into a six storey apartment block. He walked in.

There was a line of metal letter boxes inside on the right, a wide spiral staircase of polished wood at the end of the passage, a crowd of people at the bottom, looking up, talking to each other.

He passed between them. They reacted, drew away from whatever they felt. He walked up the steep circular stairs. Something was drawing him to an upper floor, he knew he had never been there, had never been in the house before.

A green door on the third landing beckoned.

He went through, into the apartment.

It was full of gendarmes, plain clothes police, flashes from a camera bulb, blood stains on the walls.

On the polished parquet floor of a sedate sitting room lay a human shape under a white sheet stained with blood in the centre where the genitals would be. Beyond, through an arch, still a part of the living room, was the body of a woman, middle aged, naked, a carving knife gripped in her right hand, her throat slit and blood coagulated round the hideous wound.

A massacre. He opened his eyes. He was back in his room, in Chantal's guest room.

He sat up. Why that scene? He knew. He didn't want to admit it, but he knew. He got up, walked out of the room and went straight to Chantal's own bedroom. She was lying on her bed in a kimono, her head resting on two pillows, her arms down her sides, her feet together.

She turned to look at him and smiled.

"You were there too," she said, "You were in my old apartment in Paris just now."

He nodded.

"I made them kill each other," she said. "I never liked them. They were very pompous, very bourgeois. It was just an experiment to see if I could will them to do it. Isn't it extraordinary the power we have?"

CHAPTER NINE

IT was dead of night. Zuke was restless. They had all experienced personal astral projection, had even experienced each other's and it had drained her of energy.

She had gone home, travelled in her imagination across the Atlantic and then across half America to Arizona, to Glendale, to her home, and she had seen her mother, in bed with a man she did not know. She had not woken them up, she had just stared at the familiar surroundings, noted the few changes which had taken place since she had left, then returned to her real self.

Chantal had asked her to try and visit somewhere she had never been before, she managed the apartment in Paris, as Warren had, an hour or so after him when everything had been cleared up and only two police officers were left in the blood-smeared living room.

She had made notes about the journeys made and compared them with Chantal, they had come to the conclusion that distance was of no consequence, long distances did not tire any more than short ones, and they were able to share where they had been.

Chantal, who had travelled a great deal, especially since her husband had died and before settling in Puerto Lucena, was therefore a fascinating source and, as Warren had humorously pointed out, their ability to astrally project within those boundaries gave a new meaning to armchair travel.

But it was frightening, for there was no control. They might be in the middle of doing something and the brain might suddenly take off and drop them unsuspectingly in a foreign environment. While swimming in the pool Zuke had found herself back at the Murcia hotel, not in the pool but in the restaurant where she had dined with Luis before the tragedy. There was no logic to it, as there was no logic to imagination. God help the psychic with a grasshopper mind.

Eventually they had gone to bed in their separate rooms. Now she was wide awake and it was three in the morning.

She felt a terrible need to be with someone, to be hugged, to be loved. She could not get the sight of her mother out of her mind, cuddling her unknown lover, smiling in her sleep. If she had reproached her in the past for being promiscuous, she now had to admit that the accusation had always been tinged with envy.

Her mother was very attractive and had always found it easy to pick up a man whenever she felt the need.

She thought she heard the door open. She stiffened. What she didn't need now was to experience another manifestation. Her nerves were too much on edge to cope.

"Sshhh. Don't put the light on."

It was Warren.

He was next to her in the dark, smelling of cologne, of tobacco, of brandy. He was naked and as he got onto the bed next to her, uninvited, the warm silkiness of his erect penis brushed against her arm.

"What are you doing?" she asked.

It was such a stupid question, and he was already on top of her quite forcefully.

"Warren!"

She objected on principal, but realised she was aroused, amused, ready for exactly this.

He said nothing but pinned her arms down,

her legs. She resisted and though slight, still a boy really, he was nervously strong and for a moment he hurt her.

She was dry, there was resistance to entry and it annoyed him, the awkward jabbing. Then he was through, suddenly, and it felt marvellous. He moved well. She put her arms round his neck, their mouths met.

It was going to be good. At long last she had him and it was going to be really good. He was naturally sensuous, as she had suspected, and he was laughing because she had eased herself into a more comfortable position.

His cologne was recognisable. Chantal's. Christ! He had probably just been with her.

The pleasure was welling up. He knew what he was doing, holding back, checking the rhythm. The delight was tortuously slow and she closed her eyes only to open them again immediately to stare at someone who had come in with a candle.

It was Chantal, standing there over them watching, nude herself.

Warren pulled out before it was over. He knelt there on the bed beside her, his huge wet erection casting a shadow on the wall.

"Suce le!" Chantal ordered.

She was like a witch, an evil sorceress but somehow beautiful with her long black hair contrasting with her so white skin.

She felt she had been through this before. Warren wasn't Warren any more, not in the candlelight. He was handsome though, desirable, with a mass of curly hair and his penis proferred a few inches from her mouth. She took it, knew what to do with it, knelt on the bed herself, over him now.

Then Chantal's arms hugged her from behind, she could feel her breasts moving against her back as she watched Warren moaning, groaning in ecstacy.

He pulled out, pushed her aside, hurled himself on Chantal who gripped him feverishly.

They were demonic, the white female clinging like a leech to the darker male, the pale legs gripping the tanned thighs, that tongue darting everywhere, the eyes manic with frenzy.

Zuke watched, she wanted to be part of it, wrestled to get between them, then, suddenly, she did not know how, he was in her again, and her face was being licked by Chantal's tongue, her whole body, licked and bitten, kissed and caressed.

It was dark, the candle had gone out, she was being covered by a liquid warmth, Warren up against her very heart and the longed for orgasm coming, enveloping her, pulling her into a fathomless abyss, arrested in its gathering speed by cushions of human feelings, smothering her, sheathing her, a fusion of bodies, a fusion of minds, a unification, a centralisation. She felt they were so tightly united that they had entered each other's very souls.

And then she lost consciousness.

When she awoke it was dawn and she found herself between them, the naked Warren, the nude Chantal in a deep sleep, she the youngest, the most vulnerable used as a catalyst, visited in her own bed and ravished.

She got off the bed cautiously, found a dressing gown and went to the kitchen.

Everything was absolutely normal. Coffee, milk, sugar. She went out to sit on the patio and looked at the fields, the sea beyond, watched the line of cars on the distant motorway that hugged the mountains.

She was alive. They had indulged in an orgy, and she had felt so good, so wanted.

At one moment it had been a revelation, the sensations that the human body could experience. She had been in a trance, aware only of the movement inside her, of the satanic shadows cast against the vaulted limestone ceiling by the flames that burnt in the massive chimney.

Where had that been? Somewhere in the past. The monks watching. The monks? A prelate in his crimson robes unbuttoned by the

nun, the nun in white looking so pure, so innocent.

And there had been that wretched youth on
the rack and the line of choir boys holding
those red hot branding irons.

She had felt a thrill as the boy had been un-
chained and then stretched over the table. She
had felt a terrible thrill. And she had listened
to the screams with some sort of delight. And
they had become her own screams of abandon-
ment.

She would wait now till the others woke up
and find comfort in their company. She would
have a bath till then, a long hot bath to wash
away the sins of the world.

She took her time ambling down the passage
to Chantal's bathroom carrying her mug of coffee. She glanced at the antique mirror on the
wall as she passed it and stopped dead.

Her reflection was her own, yet not. Staring
at herself she did not recognise Zuke, but
Chantal. She was Chantal. She looked down
and saw her delicate white feet with the carefully manicured toe nails, looked at her white
hands with long red nails which had so plea-
surably dug into the tanned male neck.

Had not last night been an experience worth
repeating?

She smiled at the reflection. Strange that
only a moment ago she should have thought

of herself as Zuke. Interesting. Yet when she had got up, made the coffee, she had left herself sleeping with Warren, had seen herself lying there curled in his arms.

She looked at the mug of coffee in her hand. She tasted it. It was sweet. She Chantal never took sugar. Zuke always did. A metamorphosis then? Had Zuke felt like having a bath, Zuke who never had a bath but always, always, a shower? Would she change into Warren and grow a phallus?

She went to the kitchen, the coffee jar was open, the sugar jar in the wrong place. She had been Zuke then. She tiptoed back into the bedroom. There were two naked figures lying on the bed, Zuke and Warren, interlaced, masculinity hugging her small feminine frame. She went up to them and touched them. They were both warm, both breathing. How could a metamorphosis take place like that?

Was it all happening in the mind? She went to the bathroom, ran the hot water, watched the mirror steam up and wiped it clean very quickly. She was not going to miss the change if it was to happen again.

In the bath she tried to go over the events of the previous night. She could not remember how she had ended up in Zuke's room, but it had been his suggestion. While lying with her in her own bed he had said that they should not leave Zuke out of it, and the thought of seeing him with the younger girl had excited her and she had deliberately let him go on ahead, then joined them, watching the movements of their lovemaking by the light of the candle.

She lay there in the hot water, happy, content, a contentment arising from something achieved, then she got out and dried herself carefully in front of the mirror.

No change.

Chantal, milky skinned, feminine, her long black hair falling over her delicate shoulders.

The materialisation was sudden and came in from the left. The apparition was old, naked, translucent, but her own height, her build, it was a bent figure, grey haired, with whispy sideburns, waxen, sallow, parchment skin, the curl of the lip not unlike Warren's, the demented eyes penetrating, a mass of white pubic hair round a long hanging member, skeletal arms, skeletal rib cage. Armando Valdez Ortega.

The reflections fused.

She touched his skin, which was her own skin, she felt the bristles on his chin, which was her chin, she threaded her fingers through the grey hair, her hair. She was Valdez. He was she. It was working, at long last it was working.

* * *

He had a pain in the back of his neck and he raised his hand to touch the scar, the weal, he reached out to touch the mirror, it was not his hand but hers, Chantal's. The glass gave no resistance and behind her, behind him, a hundred times repeated were the images of him behind her, of Chantal, of Warren, of Zuke, of himself, of Chantal, of Warren, of Zuke, of himself, endlessly repeated into infinity and when he put his arm further into the mirror the reflections fused, became one, and there was no mirror to look at, only a black rectangle and the familiar terrifying logic of limbo, with its timelessness, its colourlessness, its soundlessness.

There was nothing to touch, just the mind working, the soul with its memories. He was Warren, he was Zuke, he was himself.

He made an effort, moved himself backwards and felt the surface anew, felt the surface of the glass and the vision came back, human again, alive, naked in Chantal's bathroom. He needed a shave, he had been to bed with two women, had had a *ménage-à-trois*, despite Pippa's death, despite all his efforts to resist temptation he had done it, had behaved like some psychopath, and now felt so thirsty, so parched that he needed a cup of tea.

He went into the kitchen. Someone had already been up and about, had had breakfast, and he remembered making coffee, though he never had coffee first thing. Perhaps there hadn't been any tea, and he had been up already?

He couldn't remember. It was like a terrible hangover. Had he not just had a bath? Soaped his milky skin?

He looked down. He had no breasts, he was a man. He went quickly to Zuke's room. The girls were there, interlaced, the pale one with the dark hair, the tanned one with the blonde hair. Had he not, though, just seen himself in that position?

Valdez. It was clear again. He, Valdez Ortega had managed to reproduce himself in these three beings. He had managed it and would now be able to carry out further experiments. He was Warren Ryder, he was Zuleika, he was Chantal, and he had the knowledge of all three, and his own knowledge. He was a triple metempsychic with endless horizons, endless powers.

He left the bathroom, reacting to the feel of the hard tiles against the soles of his feet. He touched the walls, the woodwork of the furniture, he lay down on Chantal's bed.

He had achieved the impossible from limbo and now suddenly felt the incredible exhaustion of the live being.

He had experienced the feeling before through Jacinta, the ability to touch solidity. It would be uncomfortable until he had become accustomed to it, but worth it.

How long would he have on earth this time? As long as their human frames lasted, and he could be in three places at once.

Whose shape would he adapt to best? Or would he be in all three at all times? Chantal came through the door threading on her house gown, and behind her Zuke was putting on a T-shirt, and Warren behind them zipping up his jeans.

They all looked at each other and all knew at once, all knew at the very same moment, through the one person that they all were, that a fearful mistake had been made.

He had not multiplied himself threefold. He had divided his powers into three. He had not increased, but decreased his psychic potential, and the only way he could regain the strength he wanted would be by ridding himself of two of them, by destroying the weakest.

Zuke knew she was herself when she realised she was afraid. The feeling grew stronger by the hour.

As a reincarnation of Valdez she would have had more self assurance, more confidence in the future, but now she realised that as the weakest of the three metempsychics, she would be the first to be eliminated, and such a death would mean utter oblivion, for there would be no master spirit to return to in limbo. Valdez was on earth now in Warren's shape, in Chantal's shape, even a little in her own.

Though she was now part of Valdez, of Warren, of Chantal, she still wanted to survive as herself, as Zuke, and she was going to fight. She preferred her own identity and knew that the others in their true moments would want to be themselves as well, but unlike them her true moments were the norm.

It was Warren and Chantal who had started the orgy which had led to the fusion. It had not worked, the strength of the metempsychosis had been wrongly gauged. She was still one individual and she might have to kill the others in order to survive. She would do so by leaving this environment, this house, this whole area, she would do so by regaining her own strength by herself.

She looked at the objects in her room, touched them, exhorted them to move. Nothing happened.

She lay down on the bed and closed her eyes and wished herself back home in America, imagined the street where she lived, then her bedroom, then the back garden. They were lifeless images. They were forced memories, nothing more. Had she already been stripped of her psychic abilities. Had Valdez acted so swiftly?

She got up, looked at her own reflection in the mirror. She was still Zuke, and as Zuke had to get away. She had no idea what the others were doing or thinking, there was no contact, no telepathy, they were disengaged and were now three separate individuals.

She knew this, an instinct as clear as the inner knowledge that she would be the first victim if she did not protect herself.

She went across to the window and on an impulse climbed out. She crossed the yard, reached the gate in the high wall that separated Chantal's property from the neighbouring orchard, opened it slowly, slipped through and ran down the path leading to the main road where she slowed down and started walking. She had no money and only what she was dressed in. She would not thumb a lift ever again, but as she saw an old woman coming towards her, she concentrated hard, willing her to stop and give her something, a few pesetas, anything, just to prove that she had telepathic powers, that she could enter other people's minds and tell them what to do.

The woman passed her by as though she did not exist. Zuke looked at her walk away, she was so strangely dressed, like a peasant from a Goya painting, and coming down the road, which was now like an old track, was a horse and cart, another peasant with a large straw hat sitting on his load of hay.

She walked on, suspecting what was happening to her. She looked around for a telegraph pole, an electric cable, something new, something modern. Ahead there were only low whitewashed houses to be seen, no high rises, or concrete blocks, no stainless steel doorways, no cars.

She now noticed that the road she was walking on no longer had an asphalt surface softened by the burning sun: it was a dirt road of fine earth, pebbles and dust. Somewhere along the way she had stepped into the past through a time barrier.

So where was the rest of her? How would they find her now that she was in another life zone, the new Alice through the looking glass?

As she approached a crowd of gossiping women she became acutely aware that they could not see her for they did not turn round, and any group of women in any village at any time in history would surely have turned round to look at a stranger.

She passed them by, she even paused to study them, but they still did not see her. For them she did not exist. She was therefore a ghost and it then occurred to her that perhaps she was dead, that this was limbo, or that she had been reincarnated into the past. If time became meaningless after death, why had she always assumed that reincarnation hurled one into the future? And what was sudden death? Had she, while lying on the bed or when stepping out of the window been attacked and killed? How did one know when death occurred?

She turned a corner expecting to see the familiar supermarket and the two boutiques with their leather goods and expensive accessories, but of course everything was different. Quite different. There was a large open space, a square shaded by trees and on the other side was the church; bright white with new doors, straight walls, bright red tiles on the roof and a shining gold cross on its little bell tower.

What century was she in? What year? She who had never believed in the church, who had never sought sanctuary, was seeking sanctuary now.

She went in, it was familiar. She had visited the church twice, once on first arriving in the pueblo, like any tourist pretending interest in the architecture, in the religious artifacts, the second time with Chantal for Jacinta's funeral.

She was on home ground: the aisle, the chapels on either side, the altar with its ornate familiar carvings, the smell of incense and people kneeling in the pews.

It was all the same, quite beautiful, with women and children and men crowding round the font, a baptism in progress, the priest incanting, then the mention of a name . . .

"Armando Valdez Ortega . . ."

It was his christening, then? No fluke period in time, but the day of his baptism, the day the church was receiving him as a child of God? And he had spent his life denying the paternity.

Then she noticed a figure standing behind one of the church pillars looking at her, dressed quite inappropriately for the period in white jeans and a blue short-sleeved shirt.

It was Warren and, as she caught his eye, she quite inexplicably saw herself, the young American girl in equally inappropriate jeans and T-shirt, right there instead of him behind the pillar.

It was a question of survival. The girl had to be killed. The girl . . . ?

She had no time to think, she had to do it that was all, he had to do it.

He . . . ?

The walk alone had been exhausting, following Zuke, hiding behind trees, behind walls, behind buildings so that she would not see him.

Somewhere Chantal would be chasing them

both, would be thinking the same thoughts, have the same knowledge.

Survival depended on the elimination of the other two.

How? Unpremeditated murder. A scarf, strangulation. It was hardly important. He moved swiftly to the other pillar and watched Zuke dart behind the group round the font, then he saw a side door opening and closing.

She had escaped. He ran. He ran across the aisle, no one turned for no one saw him, though a few women lifted their shawls higher over their heads as though suddenly cold.

He reached the side door, was out in the narrow street, in the bright sunlight, dazzled. He went to the right. It led to a deserted square surrounded by houses with wrought iron balconies and shuttered windows. Not a soul in sight, not a sound. Midday, intense heat, stillness.

There were three exits, Zuke could have taken any one of them, but he noticed a sandal footprint in the dust, the tell-tale modern footprint.

He followed the steps, some very clear, some less so. They led him in the direction of the village fountain. He looked up ahead and stopped.

The unmistakable figure was standing there

in the middle of the road holding a revolver firmly in both hands, her feet well apart.

Chantal, in black. It wouldn't work, it couldn't work, a bullet through a psychic body, for surely that is all he was, an apparition, an imagining in his own mind, in her mind, in their shared minds.

But he was rooted, unable to move, staring at Chantal, terrified. He heard the report. He saw the violence of the recoil unexpectedly pushing her to one side. He heard the whining of the bullet as it came towards him. He saw it. He saw the little metal shell glint for a fraction of a second in the sun, before the impact hurled him backwards and he was blinded by the spattering of blood across his eyes.

She had not only found the mark, she had found the fatal mark, the very centre of his forehead.

There was no pain, just the incredible knowledge that he had lost, he who had thought himself the strongest, the most likely to survive, he who had seen himself living on as the reincarnation of Valdez Ortega because he had at last accepted the secrets of the after life. All this meant nothing. He had been annihilated as a failed part of an experiment and this meant total oblivion.

She was standing above him now, revolver in hand, an expression of astonishment on her face, not believing what she had done, and he saw other people now, a crowd, men dressed in trousers like his own, women in bright beach clothes standing, staring, gasping, pointing.

Two Guardias pushed their way through, one of them easing the revolver out of Chantal's hand. A car skidded to a halt in the middle of the square where he had bought his newspaper on the first day of his holiday, where he had bought his postcards and sent them to George and Pippa and his parents and looked forward to having dinner with the rich French woman who practised ouija with a young American girl. The square . . . Puerto Lucena . . . a small tourist resort he had enjoyed before reading the *Discourse* . . . before he had ever heard of Valdez Ortega, before . . . and he closed his eyes and entered a black tunnel, felt himself being engulfed by the darkness and realised that this sensation would be his last sensation, would be his last thought for ever.

CHAPTER TEN

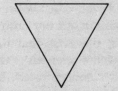

THE Guardia Civil cell was a room with a chair and a table and a bed which was not comfortable.

Chantal was aware that she would have problems, endless problems if she allowed it, but at least while here she was safe. She would claim her action to be a "crime passionnel." She would claim that Warren had been her lover and had been unfaithful. She would name Zuke as the other party in the deception involving her so that the police would bring her in for questioning, that way she would know where to find her.

It was now a matter of being patient, everything would work in her favour for she must be the central core of Valdez's experiment. She had been the first to make contact with him, had looked after his descendant and reincarnation, Jacinta, had always believed in the supernatural, and even killed Warren for his sake. He would hardly desert her now.

She realised, however, that by eliminating Warren the psychic strength of the metempsychosis was now concentrated in two people, not three, which would increase her own power but also that of Zuke.

She lay down on the bed and closed her eyes. Was Valdez within her? Was she a metempsychic with supernatural powers?

If so she could then surely convince the authorities of her innocence and turn the tables on Zuke. A name came into her mind, a name out of the blue which meant nothing to her. El Teniente Antonio Diaz.

"Antonio Diaz?" she said out loud. "A Lieutenant?" Of the Guardia Civil! She got up, banged on the door of her cell and after a while a sergeant opened up.

"I want to see Antonio Diaz," she said. "Tell him that I want to see him immediately."

The sergeant was astonished at her authoritative attitude, but all the same clicked his heels, said, *"Sí, Señora,"* and closed the door, locking it gently.

Antonio Diaz, she instinctively knew, would

be tall for a Spaniard, handsome with a thin moustache and in his early forties. She now knew that he was married and had three daughters, information from the ether which would no doubt prove useful.

He would be well disposed towards her because he knew of her, had seen her many times in the streets and restaurants and was attracted by her. It was that simple. She had to make a friend of him, work on his subconscious. He had to believe that she was innocent, that Warren, a tourist, had in fact killed himself, that she had been wrongly arrested. It was all a question of altering the view of an event in his mind. No witness, when closely cross examined, would be able to remember *exactly* what had happened. Everyone would accept that it had been a suicide. No one had been there at the moment of the accident and she could claim that the revolver was in her hand because she had picked it up from the ground where it had fallen.

The key rattled in the lock and the sergeant opened the door wide. Antonio Diaz stepped in, tall, with a thin moustache, looking exactly as she had imagined him.

He shook her by the hand and apologised profusely. Two witnesses whom he had just been questioning claimed that they had seen the incident, the accident, the tragedy and he was satisfied that the poor demented man had shot himself in front of the church while the balance of his mind was unsound. It had nothing to do with her, she had been quite wrongly accused, wrongly detained and was free to leave forthwith. He hoped she would forgive his men for doing what they thought had been their duty.

She walked out into the bright sunlight, smiling to herself. The world, it seemed, could be at her feet.

The sergeant was waiting in the courtyard for her and accompanied her to a staff car. He opened the door for her and gave instructions to the driver to take her home.

So things were beginning to work out for her. There was just Zuke to deal with which would be no great problem, though she seemed to have no inner information about her whereabouts. There was no image in that quarter, no ideas at all where she might be hiding.

Was she out of range? Or was there a self defence mechanism in action within them both?

If she could know where Zuke was, then Zuke presumably would know where she was. The thought was strong and she felt confident that she need have no fears.

The Guardia Civil staff car drew up outside

her villa, the driver got out, opened the door for her, and saluted her as she stepped out.

It made her feel important, it was the first indication she had of what it would be like to be so, it was a way of life that she would adapt to very easily, very naturally.

In the house there was an unexpected feeling of uncertainty, which unsettled her. She cautiously checked every room and searched the garden, but there was nothing unusual to be seen. All was in order.

She changed her clothes, choosing a loose yellow kaftan from her well stocked cupboard, went to the kitchen to pour herself out a cold beer, then went to lie down on her favourite sofa to relax in her own pleasant surroundings. She would now, of course, be able to afford a larger place if she wanted it, she would probably be able to purchase a very large villa, more secluded with better views; she would be able to travel, she would be able to spend. Her newly acquired powers would first of all make her a fortune, then bring her fame. Then she might put her talents to the benefit of mankind.

She might well return to Paris and take it by storm. Madame Chantal Daubigny, Legion d''Honeur.

She looked across the room at the ouija table and the crystal glass. It seemed to be beckoning to her, but she decided not to make any contacts till Zuke had been disposed of. She had a feeling, nothing more, an intuition that Zuke might well home in on her through it.

As she let out a deep sigh of satisfaction at the whole turn of events, an unexpected phrase came into her mind.

"Like a lamb to the slaughter."

And she had a clear image of Zuke.

"Zuke . . . a lamb?" She said out loud, and she turned on hearing a noise in the hallway. It frightened her. There was someone out there and no one could have got in without a key.

She stood up, edged her way to the corner and saw a figure coming towards her.

Zuke, naked, walking slowly, steadily, her eyes fixed, staring in front of her, arms rigid down her sides. It was as though she were sleep walking, as though in a trance.

The girl passed right by her, like an automaton, like a robot, steered herself straight for one of the kitchen dresser drawers from which she took out the deadliest and sharpest carving knife. She held it in her right hand and, as though it were a presentation sword of honour, she lay the flat of the blade across her left hand.

Now she came towards Chantal. Like a lamb to the slaughter, bringing its own murderous instrument of death with which to be sacrificed.

Chantal stood quite still watching the girl approaching. Zuke stared right ahead, with expressionless eyes. There was no feeling there, no self pity, no fear, no sensitivity, no life. Her mind then was already dead?

It was simply a question of terminating her physical life, of doing Valdez's bidding, for he must have sent her.

Zuke stopped a foot or so before her and proffered the knife.

Chantal slowly reached out for it—and realised too late that she had been deceived.

It was terribly quick. Zuke tightened her grip on the handle, raised the knife, flicked it up and across, and the blade cut deep into Chantal's throat not once but several times, a series of slick, deadly incisions. She was the lamb.

The pain was sharp, like a sting, and then she felt numb and saw the blood gushing down her dress, spurting out on Zuke's nakedness, falling like heavy rain drops on the marble floor.

A faintness overwhelmed her, she lost her equilibrium, saw her own hands, wet and red, reaching for a chair, staining the sacred white upholstery, smearing the white walls.

She was crossing and recrossing the room, trying to find an anchor, trying to find something to hold on to. Zuke had psychically been the strongest, and had led her to believe that she was the slaughterer when all the time she had been planning the kill and leading her to it.

"Zuke . . ." Chantal cried out.

The name did not even form on her lips. There was only a fearful guttural sound bubbling in her blood-flooded throat.

There was no pain, no feeling of falling, no feelings at all, just the floor, the pale marble floor against her cheek bone and an awareness that very soon it would all be over, totally over, no limbo, no reincarnation.

Obliteration. Total extinction. She felt her brain palpitating. Saw the jelly-like cells quiver in their death throes. She was in there, inside the skull cavity where it was dark and black and friendless . . . and then it enveloped her.

Eternal oblivion.

Zuke stared at the bloody corpse till its heaving spasms stopped, then she turned on her heels and walked out onto the patio.

The feeling was of accomplishment, of relief and of victory.

The experiment, started in 1872, had gone very wrong, but it had now been adjusted. Armando Valdez Ortega was one with the young Zuke of Glendale, Arizona. In a few moments, when everything had had time to settle, the full reincarnation, the complete metempsychic would have abundant supernatural powers and knowledge.

She was surprised how content she felt, how confident. It had not occurred to her, before the change, that a psychic state of mind would be an advantage, she had only seen it in terms of the unknown, the uncontrollable. But of course it was hers and she could do with it what she wished.

She dived into the pool and washed away the spots of Chantal's blood which had spattered her breasts and legs. Floating on her back in the water reminded her of her dive in the hotel pool with Luis and his parents-in-law looking on. Jacinta had beckoned to her then, had appeared as a ghost in the car some hours before, but as a metempsychic she had not had the earthly education, the sophistication, which Valdez obviously wanted. He had no doubt picked on her in desperation, finding no other suitable subject.

Well now he had an intelligent being who would know how to make full use of her new gifts.

She climbed up the aluminum ladder, lay down on the beach mattress and let the hot sun dry her.

It had been so easy, deceiving Chantal, she had been so sure of herself.

And poor Warren, he had had no idea of

Chantal's intentions. It had been like watching a gunfight in a western, only one of the cowboys hadn't been armed.

She was alone again, Zuke the traveller, the world her oyster, with a difference. This time she didn't mind the solitude one bit.

Too hot now, she got up and walked back into the living room, side stepping the body, and to the kitchen to make herself an iced coffee.

There were quite a number of questions she wanted answered of course, the main one being whether she was entirely on her own, or whether Valdez or Duero were going to impose duties on her.

No doubt everything would come to her gradually. Certainly for the next few days, till she felt settled, she would stay here, and to do so comfortably she would have to get rid of the corpse. How best to do that?

Dispose of it herself or have the authorities do it for her? El Teniente Antonio Diaz again! She hadn't met him herself, but knew all about him, or her Valdez half did.

She moved to Chantal's bedroom and lay down on the bed.

"Antonio Diaz," she said aloud, laughing, "I call on you to come and collect the body of another suicide."

Then she knew, she just knew, that what

she had to do was report the death in person at the Guardia Civil. They would do the rest, but she was not going to be immune from the problems of the society she was living in.

Metempsychic or not, she was going to continue living as an adult human on earth, and as such would have to suffer the disadvantages if she wanted to enjoy the privileges.

She got dressed, aware as she did so that somehow she would no longer have financial problems. If she had psychic powers she would be able to put them to good use and earn money.

New clothes, new image, new life. Who would inherit Chantal's villa? Warren's London flat?

If it depended on someone's judgment, she knew she could sway that. Her power was over the minds of decision makers and from now on all decisions would be in her favour.

She found the keys to Chantal's car in the pocket of one of her dresses. She went straight there without thinking about it, as though she had known where they were all the time.

She drove down to the Guardia Civil and asked for Teniente Antonio Diaz. She was shown into his office where he sat at a large desk with a picture of King Juan Carlos on the wall behind him.

He stood up, shook her hand, suggested she should sit down.

"La Señora Chantal Daubigny is dead," she said straight out. "I have just found her in her kitchen with her throat cut."

After displaying shock and asking for details, the Lieutenant opened a file which was in front of him and looked her straight in the eyes.

"I don't know whether you are aware of this, but your name and hers are connected with five deaths in the past few weeks. This makes six."

She said nothing.

"Have you any explanation?"

"Do you believe in the supernatural?" she asked him.

"No, but I believe in the existence of drugs, financial gain through drugs and madness through drugs."

The obvious down to earth conclusion. "I will have to detain you," he added.

"On what grounds?"

"I think you could be classed as a murder suspect."

"Have I the right to see a lawyer?"

"Eventually."

Six deaths, and he hadn't included Warren's wife or the boy on the motorbike. Did she have power?

How was it that she had walked in to report a suicide and he was going to arrest her without any evidence at all that she was guilty. A report had clearly been filed on her which had reached his office, but that did not give him the right to lock her up.

What if she told him the truth and demonstrated it?

"The death of my friends here have nothing to do with drugs. You are following a totally wrong line of enquiry. The truth is that I am a psychic, that Señora Daubigny and Señor Ryder were psychics and that we are in contact with supernatural powers which occasionally turn against us."

The Lieutenant leaned well back in his chair and smiled at her and picked his teeth with the end of a match. "You can prove that, *chica*?"

The anger welled up.

His male chauvinist contempt for a foreign girl's wishful fantasies amused him, and she found that unacceptable.

"In the next few minutes," she said, "one of your men will come in here complaining of unbearable pains in the lungs. He will then collapse and die of heart failure."

Antonio Diaz looked at her for quite a moment, leaned forward and reached for his telephone. He did not have to say anything to her for her to understand that he had decided that she was demented.

She watched him as he waited for the operator to answer, tapping his fingers on the desk.

Then there was a loud knock on the door, it opened and one of the older Guardias staggered in pressing his arms tightly against his chest.

"Señor . . ."

It was quick. He fell headlong against a filing cabinet to crumble on the floor gasping for air before twitching in a series of death throes which horrified the Lieutenant.

Zuke stood up and, stepping over the body, turned to Antonio Diaz.

"I will be at Señora Daubigny's villa, should you want me." She left.

So she had the power to kill. She walked out of the station into the bright sunlight and paused on the entrance steps to collect her thoughts.

Maybe she had been a little rash, a little too impatient to test her abilities. With a file already recording five deaths involving her, the addition of a Guardia Civil officer would not help. If the lieutenant believed her he would also see her as a threat, and threats could be disposed of, leaving the question of why to be answered afterwards.

She would have to be careful, she was not

invincible, and if she was to die herself then to what eternity would she be doomed?

She drove slowly back by way of the beach road because she wanted to look at the sea, and when she arrived at the villa six officers were already in the house, staring at Chantal's stiffening body, the blood coagulated black now, ugly, unpleasant.

One of them took her statement as others went about their business reconstructing the tragedy for their report.

"I walked into this living room an hour or so before I reported her death and found her lying there in a pool of blood, holding the knife as you see."

Valdez had been garotted for murder. Whatever had made her think she would be safe from the law?

They asked her to collect a few necessary belongings and accompany them back to the station.

She made no objection, did not argue, simply asked if she could go to the bathroom and was allowed to.

She locked the door, turned and faced the mirror, holding down a fear that was beginning to creep up on her, a fear that she would lose, that the authorities would imprison her, that perhaps she was mad and that everything that had happened was lunatic fantasy.

She stared at her reflection. Was it only this morning that she had seen herself turn into Chantal, then Valdez, then Warren?

It seemed such a very long time ago. She took off her clothes.

The apparition came in from the left like an aura to join her own. It was familiar, her other self, Valdez the old man, the bent figure with grey hair.

But there was another. Behind. Taller. More sinister. A white figure with long slender limbs and a pointed face, an aquiline nose and narrowing eyes.

It beckoned. It was asking her to step forward, to step through the mirror.

She reached out to touch the surface of the glass, but could not, for there was no longer any surface, the mirror was space, the mirror was an open door to a void.

Somewhere in the distance she heard a violent banging on the door. The noise of urgency egged her on. She stepped forward.

Oh God it was fearful!

It was like being sucked into a vacuum and with every part of her body unbearably painful, and the images of agony coming towards her, hideous, revolting faces screamed, open mouths howled, eyes hung from gouged orbits, torn fingers like tentacles reached out to scratch her, bowels, lengths of intestines curled about her, bubbles of sickly blood burst around her, and she was hurtled through black space, then held back, a tight metallic ring tightening round her throat and a sharp point inserting itself between her vertebrae behind her neck.

Death? The garotte again?

She stopped moving in the soundlessness. The grip was released and she felt herself floating down slowly and entered a fog of whiteness. She descended into a vault where emasculated men were hanging by their arms from chains bolted to the walls.

Fifteen young men, every one of them emasculated, and it was she who was responsible.

She was there, in the centre of the room, kneeling in prayer, dressed in the finest crimson robes, attended by two choir boys in white, both holding crucifixes above her head.

But she was not herself. She was Duero.

Double doors behind her burst open and a figure in black entered followed by some ten helmeted soldiers in green and black uniforms carrying pikes and swords.

There was no mercy.

The accusing finger, the sentence without trial, the brutish soldiers grabbing the vestments and rudely tearing them off, the grabbing, the knives, the slashing, the slicing, a torturous, painful death in the very manner she had inflicted on her victims.

As Duero she had sworn that she would return, that she would find a way and return from death to haunt those who had conspired against her.

And this was now achieved. She was Duero. She was his reincarnation.

He had used Valdez to return and foil the rules of the infinite and now he was back.

The fog clouded in and she felt herself moving on slowly, gathering speed till she saw the wall ahead, a black wall in the blackness which she could not avoid.

She was hurled against it head on, paralysing every nerve in her body, then she lost her awareness of everything.

She opened her eyes to find herself in strange yet familiar surroundings. A double bed, a mattress, no sheets, a view from the window of a town garden.

Fitted carpets, comforts, mustiness, dust, pine furniture, a short corridor leading to a sitting room with an abundance of house plants, a worn sofa.

A pile of letters on the kitchen table confirmed where she was.

She had escaped them, the Guardia, by a distance of some 1,500 miles.

A psychic projection. Herself whole. A travel

in time, in space, through Valdez's execution, through Duero's hideous death.

She was alive. Unique.

Exhausted she slumped down in the sofa and stared at her surroundings, at herself. Her naked body was scratched, bloody, as though she had been through a no man's land of thorn bushes and barbed wire, dragged through mounds of powdered glass, pulled along hard, hot desert sands. But she had survived.

In front of her was a television set. She leaned forward, switched it on.

There was a news item about a siege at an airport, another hi-jacking, two hundred innocent passengers held by political terrorists.

A telescopic lens focused on a masked man inside the plane, another telescopic lens focused on shock troops in the long grass. The whole world was watching, thanks to satellites, the whole word was watching, waiting, anticipating a disaster.

She closed her eyes and concentrated on the image of the terrorist in the plane. The mask, the faint outline of the tense mouth.

"Pull the trigger and let all hell loose," she whispered.

The television set crackled.

She opened her eyes wide. The camera was trained on the fuselage which had suddenly burst into flames, hurling wreckage up in the air to crash down on the tarmac. A hole now appeared in the side, shock troops advanced. Panic, chaos, death, it was all there for her to see along with the millions of other viewers, all there within a framed space of so many square inches.

Had she the power to terminate life at such a distance, of willing men to kill each other?

Duero had done nothing else but destroy. Valdez had been his puppet, she was their re-incarnation, but with whose character, whose morals?

She heard a sound behind her, a key being inserted in the lock. She turned.

A woman was standing in the doorway shocked into silence at seeing her. The shock was not at her presence in the flat, but at her nakedness.

"I was just relaxing after my journey," she explained, "I'm a friend of Warren's, he said I could use the apartment for a week or two."

"Oh . . . that's all right, I'm sorry to have disturbed you."

And the lady left as discreetly as she had come in.

On the television the cameras happily panned the carnage. All aboard the plane were dead, seventeen of the shock troops had been killed, all the hi-jackers had been eliminated.

She had seen such scenes before, so many

scenes like it before, of war, of destruction, but it had never occurred to her that the influence behind the lawlessness might emanate from an evil spirit such as herself.

And who would ever suspect?